MEMORIES DIE LAST

Tim Smith

AmErica House
Baltimore

© 2002 by Tim Smith.

First printing

ISBN: 1-59129-242-5
PUBLISHED BY
AMERICA HOUSE BOOK PUBLISHERS
www.publishamerica.com
Baltimore

Printed in the United States of America

Dedication

To my family and friends who encouraged me to take the big step in writing this story and all those that followed. This is just the beginning, and may we all find the real elusive target – happiness.

Acknowledgments

While writing this story, I realized that while I had the basic ingredients for a good yarn, some of the technical aspects were foreign to me. Luckily, I had the good fortune to have friends with law enforcement backgrounds who were willing and able to provide excellent insights into the areas with which I was unfamiliar (thank you, Keith and Jim). I was also fortunate enough to work with two colleagues with solid literary credentials, as well as having a family member with a degree in English Literature, all of whom gave some very good suggestions on how to improve the finished product and provide a sense of balance to the story (a tip of the hat to Sue, Teresa and Jeff). I was further blessed to have other friends and family members who gave a unique perspective on how to develop the relationship between the two main characters: "Don't let these two get married, and turn up the heat whenever they're together!" To all of you, I say, "Thank You," for your assistance and support – and will the real 'Felicia' please step forward?

Tim Smith

- *One* -

The late afternoon sun was falling over Key Largo, reflecting on the water's surface. The bright blue of the ocean mixed with the orange tint of sunset to create a beautiful, multi-hued sight. A gentle breeze blew in from the Gulf of Mexico as seagulls lazily flapped their wings in almost symmetrical patterns over the harbor, swooping lower with each pass, hoping to catch dinner. Yachts slowly cruised into the marina, their masters having finished another day of rest and recreation, ready to put their expensive toys away until some other time. The deck alongside the water also had a steady stream of people, most armed with cameras, taking pictures of the daily show the setting sun was putting on for all to enjoy.

Nick Seven took in this routine ritual from his usual vantage point at Calhoun's Yacht Club: corner table off the bar, near the window, always set for two but usually occupied by one, where he could observe with bemused curiosity the comings and goings of the rich and not-so-famous. He never tired of watching the activity against the backdrop of the most beautiful sunsets in the world, and some nights proved more entertaining than others – seeing which flavor of the week went out for a day of boat rocking with the old man who owned the brokerage firm while his wife was away, seeing who would walk off the boats, and who would have to be carried off by one of the boys from the Yacht Club. Some evenings, this was better than television.

Nick had his usual glass of bourbon and ginger ale sitting in front of him, along with a smoldering cigarette in the ashtray. All around him he could hear the clinking of glasses and the low-key chatter of drinkers and diners, along with the sounds of soft jazz from the club's sound system. On nights like this, he often reflected on the circumstances that brought him to this point in his life – but not too deeply. Some memories are better left alone. Nick's life had been like a rollercoaster ride through hell and back. Here he was, a veteran of Army Intelligence who mustered out with the rank of Major, obtained a degree in Law, then joined the CIA when they had come knocking on his door. There, he had labored as a field agent for a dozen years, specializing in international terrorism, until something made him give it all up and walk away. That's when he parlayed his pension and a Royal Flush into ownership of Calhoun's, a popular bar and restaurant located on the bay. It had proven to be a shrewd move (as if he ever made any other kind). The place was already popular with the local crowd and hordes of tourists who flocked to the Keys to catch those sunsets and the occasional fish . After taking up residence, rumors buzzed through the local community about Nick's past, making him a mysterious figure, but he never discussed it with anyone, not even Kristine, his on-again/off-again companion. In the beautiful setting of southern Florida, Nick had finally found his concept of paradise. He did, however, resist the urge to rename the club "Rick's" or "Bogart's".

Nick often pondered why he had made the move in the first place, sometimes wistfully thinking that he actually missed the action of being in the field, tracking down leads that would ultimately bring down someone bent on making a name for themselves by blowing up a few landmarks. But then, just like a bucket of ice water in the face, he would remember why he got out. After eleven years of globetrotting, where he had distinguished himself as the poster boy for always getting your man and not taking any bullshit from the brass, he had requested an assignment at Quantico, training new agents for their day on the firing line. He was good at preparing these fresh-faced recruits for the challenge of confronting some misguided soul, convinced that they were committing mass murder or suicide in the name of Allah, or some asshole named Saddam. He soon came to realize, however, that he didn't belong in the classroom. But that wasn't the real reason Nick Seven had called it quits.

* * *

A few hundred miles and a lifetime away, Daniel Currey was sitting in his office at CIA headquarters in Langley, Virginia. The office itself wasn't much – slightly smaller than the Astrodome, with a desk that you could probably land a light plane on. Across from him sat Gene Brodie, the Bureau Chief in charge of Domestic Affairs. They had been reviewing some intelligence reports of weapons trading in New York that could have some connection with recent domestic terrorist activities.

Currey leaned forward, resting his forearms on his desk. He slowly, rhythmically tapped a pencil on the desktop while thinking.

"Just doesn't sound like the Iraqis' style," he finally said. "Too clandestine, too covert. Historically they've always struck hard, then run for cover, bragging about their deeds to CNN when they were tucked safely away in their bomb shelters."

"I agree," said Brodie, "but how else do you explain this stockpiling of arms and munitions that our black market informers have reported? And what about this recent rash of bombings and attacks throughout the country? You think there's some connection to the IRA?"

Currey shook his head.

"No, I don't think that's it either," he said. "They typically have their own suppliers in the UK or South America. They don't need to come to America to buy street weapons. Plus, they usually limit their activities to the United Kingdom." He paused for a minute before finally speaking again. "I'm afraid we're getting a wake-up call from someone we haven't heard from in a while."

"Who?"

Currey paused again, and resumed tapping the pencil for a few moments. He suddenly stopped, stared hard into Brodie's eyes and responded to his question.

"Lavender."

"But that's impossible!" Brodie responded. "Lavender's been dead for nearly five years."

"Are you certain about that?"

"As certain as I can be. I practically watched as Nick

Seven killed him during that raid in London."

"How can we be sure it was Lavender? After all, he made an art out of cheating death for years."

"The person I saw laying in a heap in that back alley with three slugs from Nick's service revolver had Lavender's face, his fingerprints, even his dental records matched. No, it has to be someone else."

"Everything you mentioned could have been faked," Currey argued. "The Russians had doubles for their agents during the Cold War, we tried it ourselves, and science and medicine have come a long way since then. Even someone's DNA can be tinkered with now, so the possibility definitely exists that it was someone other than Miles Lavender who was killed in that raid."

"I suppose it's possible," Brodie responded thoughtfully, stroking his chin with his right thumb and forefinger. "But even if it is, where do we go from here?"

"We have to find the one man who knew Lavender better than anyone – someone who knows his habits, his hangouts, his favorite foods, even the brand of whiskey he drinks. Someone who can get into his head and think like he does. We need Nick Seven."

This time it was Brodie's turn to shake his head in a vehement "no".

"Nick will never go for it," Brodie said.

"How can you be so sure?"

"I was his partner and the closest thing he had to a friend for nearly a dozen years. Yes, he knows Lavender, but I know Nick Seven."

"Do you know where he is now?" Currey asked.

Brodie paused for a moment, not sure if he should

answer, then finally realizing that the Old Man could find out whether he responded or not.

"He owns a yacht club down on Key Largo, one of those places where the nouveau riche like to hang out. Had it ever since he quit the agency, been quite successful, even accepted by the locals. No ties to anything except the club, although he dabbles a little as a photographer in his spare time. Not even a significant other to speak of, just a local gal that he hangs out with once in a while."

"Gene, you and Nick Seven headed the best field team we had operating in Europe at that time," Currey said. "Four people – you, Nick, Artie Sawyer, and Felicia Hagens."

Brodie smiled wistfully and slowly nodded his head.

"Team Seven, they called us," he said.

"Team Seven took on the worst the enemy could throw at us, and together you put the fear of God in the hearts of a lot of terrorists," Currey continued. "Now there are only three of you left, since Sawyer was taken out by that sniper in Beirut last year. We have to appeal to Seven's sense of honor, his duty to his country, anything."

"It won't do you any good, " Brodie stated. "I know Nick Seven, and I know just what he'll tell you: 'Kiss my royal Scottish ass.'"

"I know," Currey said. "That's why I'm not going to ask him – YOU are."

"Oh, swell," Brodie muttered.

Currey opened a drawer, withdrew a small packet of papers, and tossed them across the desk to Brodie.

"Better go home and get packed," he said. "Your plane

leaves for Miami in two hours, and there's a car waiting for you at Hertz."

Brodie picked up the packet, reluctantly got up from his chair, and moved towards the door.

"Oh, Gene, one more thing," Currey said. "Do what you have to, say what you have to, but I want Seven."

"I may have to lie to him, you know," Brodie replied.

"Well, it's not like you haven't done that before, is it?" Currey said with a grin.

Brodie scowled at his boss, then left the office.

* * *

The dinner crowd was holding fort at Calhoun's. Brodie surveyed the well-dressed landscape before him. He'd never seen so much pastel and khaki in one place before, and now knew how Ralph Lauren and Tommy Hilfiger stayed in business.

He approached the bar, and finally caught the eye of the bartender, a young man of Cuban descent.

"Yes, sir?"

"I'm looking for Nick Seven," Brodie said. "He been in tonight?"

"The Chief don't take visitors unless they got an appointment," the bartender replied. "You got an appointment?"

"No," responded Brodie, "but if you tell Mr. Seven that his Uncle Sammy is in town for a visit, I think he'll see me."

"Uncle Sammy? The Chief ain't got no Uncle named Sammy. Got one named Archie, a cousin named Moe, and a hot-lookin' aunt named Conchita, but no Sammy."

"Tell him anyway," Brodie insisted.

"OK, man," the bartender replied. "It's your funeral."

The young man disappeared for a few minutes, then came back.

"I don't know which part of the family tree you fell out of, man," he said, "but he'll see you. Follow me."

Brodie followed the young man to Nick's table. Nick didn't get up from his seat, or say a word. He just leaned back in his captain's chair, his right leg crossed over his left, his left elbow resting on the arm of the chair, with his left hand cupping his chin, a look of amusement on his face. He slowly looked Brodie over, first up and down, then bore into his eyes with a look that cut right to his soul.

"Hello, Nick," Brodie said, extending his right hand. "Been a long time."

Nick paused a few seconds before accepting the right hand of friendship, and almost reluctantly shook hands with his former partner. He then motioned to the empty chair, and Brodie sat down.

"You want anything, Chief?" asked the bartender.

"Another bourbon and ginger, Raul," he answered. "Plus whatever my 'Uncle' is having."

"I hear you make a mean Cuba Libra here," Brodie said, as Raul went back to the bar.

Nick was still maintaining the same pose, and staring at Brodie, but the amused look from before was now mixed with curiosity. Finally, he spoke. "Uncle Sammy," he said, drawing out each syllable. "How original."

"Well, I didn't think you'd remember any of the old

passwords," said Brodie.

"So how are things in the real world these days?" asked Nick, still not sure how to react to the sudden appearance of his old friend from another lifetime. "Still overthrowing dictatorships and blaming it on the Iraqis, or are we trying to re-ignite the Cold War?"

"Oh, about the same," Brodie answered. "They try to kill us, we try to kill them, then point the finger at each other. You heard about Artie Sawyer, didn't you?"

Nick nodded his head slowly, not changing his expression.

"Poor bastard," Brodie said. "Otherwise, nothing's changed. Except for you – you look great!"

"Cut the crap," Nick said. "You didn't come all the way down here at government expense just to tell me that the sea air agrees with me. What do you want, Gene?"

Brodie lowered his head in contemplation for a moment, choosing his next words carefully. Finally, he raised his head and looked Seven in the eye.

"We're in trouble, Nick. Deep trouble. We need your help."

Nick narrowed his eyes until they were almost a squint. He chose his next utterance carefully, too.

"Kiss my royal Scottish ass," he responded.

Brodie chuckled softly to himself.

"I told Currey that's what you'd say."

"By the way, how is the old chair-polisher?" asked Nick.

"Worried," Brodie answered. "Worried that he might be out of a job soon."

"Why? The government's always going to need spooks

like you to plot against some foreign power, then point your finger at Castro and say, 'He did it!'"

"It's the budget, more than anything. Don't you follow the news?"

"Nah. It's too damn depressing."

"This new moron in the White House isn't satisfied with cutting the defense budget and closing military installations, now he's got the carving knife out for The Agency, too."

"That shouldn't be too hard for you guys to get around. Just have the Federal Bureau of Intimidation plant a wire in the Oval Office and start a file. It worked for Hoover."

Brodie paused, took a deep breath, and tried the sales pitch.

"The thing is, Nick," he began, "we're up against something that's got us stumped. Someone, or some group, is stockpiling weapons and munitions like the Palestinians are already in Jersey. There have been a few random attacks, nothing we can piece together, with the promise of more to come." He paused and stared hard at Seven. "Terrorism has come home to the land of the free, Nick, and we need someone with your experience. We need to reactivate Team Seven."

Nick looked at Brodie for a long time, taking the occasional drag on his cigarette, and sipping his drink. He was remembering all the times they had been through – raids on terrorist compounds, dodging bullets and grenades in Beirut, going undercover, freeing hostages and political prisoners, fighting over various women, consoling each other over the men they lost in battle. He was also thinking of one moment in time in particular, but quickly purged the thought from his memory.

"I see you haven't lost your talent for blowing smoke up someone's ass," Nick finally said, "but there's nothing you can say that will convince me to get involved again. I walked away from the life once, and I intend to stay out. I also don't believe that The Agency, with all its resources and manpower, needs an ex-gunslinger like me to solve its problems. Now, if you'll excuse me," he said while rising, "I've got a business to run and rich customers to rub elbows with." He extended his right hand, which Brodie shook. "It was nice seeing you again."

Nick turned and started to walk away. Brodie spoke one last word: "Lavender."

Nick stopped cold, slowly turned around, and faced Brodie.

"Nice try," Nick said. "'A' for effort. But if resurrecting a dead assassin is the best you can do, you need to go back to spy school."

"We think he's alive, Nick," Brodie said, with all the conviction he could muster. "Everything that's happened so far has all his trademarks."

Nick slowly walked back to the table and resumed his seat. He stared at Brodie with a look that was a cross between disbelief and disgust. His face suddenly turned to stone, and his eyes took on a hollow look. When he finally spoke, it was almost like a disembodied voice coming from a tomb – no emotion, only sound.

"Lavender is dead," Nick began. "I killed him. You identified the body. Three shots, all on target. The first two killed him, and the third was for –"

Nick stopped short. It was like he was reciting the story

from rote, repeating it for a board of inquiry for the twelfth time.

"That's it and that's all," he continued in the same monotone. "I even went to the funeral to be sure he was sent back to hell. It's not him."

"I agree it's a stretch," Brodie said. "But it's all we have. Either it's Lavender reincarnated, or a damn good copycat. Isn't there anything you can do to help us out, Nick?"

Nick said nothing. His mind was suddenly racing, going off in a hundred different directions all at once.

What if I didn't really get him? What if it wasn't him, only a stand-in? What if he's still out there? If I killed the wrong man, then I still owe one to –

Nick lowered his head slightly, and closed his eyes for a moment, thinking.

"Look, Gene," he said at length, "I can't just jump back into the game after being out for several years. I may have lost my edge."

"Not you," said Brodie. "I checked you out, kept tabs on you. You still work out five times a week, can bench press two hundred pounds, and you're licensed to carry a gun, which in this state means you have to qualify on the pistol range. Don't jerk me, Nick."

Nick said nothing, so Brodie continued.

"Nice place," he said, looking around the room. "I'll bet the customers here know nothing about your past. You were always tight-lipped when you had to be. How about that society dame you shack up with? What's her name – Kristine? You know, the one who stands to inherit that seat on the board of Coca Cola when her old man kicks?

She really know anything about you?"

Nick still said nothing, but the squint and glare returned to his eyes.

"Funny, though, how you never get your picture in the papers when you two go to all those society bashes," Brodie continued. "Even though you always looked great in a tux, one might say that you're camera-shy, or that you're just afraid someone might recognize your face and come to settle an old grudge. Oh, well – I guess some people are destined to stay in the background, aren't they? I wonder what she, or any of your rich patrons and friends would say if they knew how many men you've killed or the grisly details of some of the less-than-tasteful things you did in your previous life?"

Nick was still silent, but glaring harder.

"I'll bet they wouldn't think too much of that great guy who runs the local yacht club and hobnobs with their wives and virginal daughters," Brodie continued. "Of course, don't get me wrong, Nick, I'd never spoil this great thing you have going here, but as you know, word has a way of getting around."

After another long pause, Nick raised his right hand, placed two fingers on his forehead and gave Brodie a mock salute.

"My compliments, partner," he said. "I'll get back to you."

Brodie stood up.

"My plane leaves Miami tomorrow morning at 11:15," he said. "I'm staying at the Holiday Inn. Call me."

- *Two* -

If only…

Two of the most powerful words in the English language, especially when one is second-guessing their actions. Nick was starting each thought with these words now.

Calhoun's had closed and the help had all gone home. Only Nick remained, still sitting at his usual table. He often sat in the darkened bar after closing, sometimes watching the inlet lit by the moon, sometimes just thinking. This was one of those times. He had retrieved a bottle of his favorite Scotch from his private stash, the stuff he only brought out for special occasions, or when he had something on his mind. He sat at the small glass-topped bamboo table, a candle burning in the center, a cigarette in his hand, and a glass with ice and Scotch in front of him. "The Famous Grouse Scotch Whiskey." In the light streaming in from the marina outside, Nick held the bottle and looked at the drawing of the red-feathered grouse on the label, reading the logo next to the coat of arms – "By appointment to Her Majesty, The Queen." Nick had become fond of this particular brand of Scotch when he worked in Great Britain years ago on assignment.

Nick's cigarette had burned down, so he took another

one from the box on the table. He tapped the butt end a few times on his gold cigarette lighter, then lit up. He stared for a few minutes at the lighter in the palm of his right hand. It was engraved with his initials on one side, and the seven of hearts on the other. It held great meaning for Nick. The lighter had been a special gift from someone who was also very special.

Nick puffed his cigarette and looked at the bottle of Grouse sitting on the table in the flickering of the candlelight. He picked up his glass of Scotch and gently tapped it on the bottle.

"To you, babe," he softly said. "All the best."

He took a sip of his drink and sat back in his chair, thinking about something he hadn't dared to think about in years. Seeing Brodie earlier and listening to what he had to say made Nick recall the time he spent in Great Britain.

In a way, he was happier stationed in England, but only because of one thing: a girl named Gwyn (short for "Gwyndolyn"). She was a Scottish girl, the product of a rare blind date arranged by a co-worker in the London office. Nick was always wrapped up in his work, and had never had that much time for socializing with the opposite sex. Not that there weren't women available to him when he wanted them – he just never took the time to even think about a commitment, or anything beyond a casual fling or one-nighter. But there was something about this girl – something at once charming and defiant, with a biting wit that clicked with his own aggressive personality. She was petite, but everything was in wonderful proportion, backed up with a hearty laugh and eyes that seemed to say,

"I dare you not to fall in love with me." It was a challenge Nick Seven couldn't pass up.

It had been a case of instant attraction for both of them. Gwyn was beautiful, and Nick couldn't keep his hands off of her. Even when things began to get serious, Nick resisted, knowing what the life of a field operative in his business was like – here today, dead tomorrow. He had explained this to Gwyn, but she didn't care. She knew what she was getting into, and what she wanted. He never forgot her words when he finally popped the question: "Only if you marry me in Scotland." They were wed a few weeks later. That's when Gwyn had given Nick the gold lighter as a wedding gift. She called it his good luck charm. Nick never went anywhere without it.

If only...

The first few months were glorious, heady times for both of them. Nick was able to stay in London, where he was given an important assignment: there was a new name on the terrorist horizon, Miles Lavender, an ex-patriate Brit with a devious mind and nasty temper who was making the Irish Republican Army look like a group of peace demonstrators. Lavender's motives were hardly altruistic: the IRA had found him to be a loose cannon, kicked him out, and now he was a mercenary, for sale to the highest bidder. The team knew that his customers included the Libyans, Colombians and the Russian Mafia. Lavender's specialties included running guns, bombings, kidnap for ransom, torture, and other assorted acts of mayhem. Sometimes he even waived his fee for such services, experiencing a perverse joy out of inflicting pain and suffering on others. The fact that he also spoke several languages fluently made it harder to keep up with him, but Nick and his team kept searching.

Nick had taken a special interest in Lavender. Aside from being an assignment, Nick knew he had to stop the renegade terrorist after he saw some of the victims he left in his wake. One of them had been the twelve-year-old daughter of a member of the British Parliament, who had been abducted and held for ransom. The girl's father quickly paid the ten thousand pounds Lavender had demanded, but Lavender hadn't kept his promise that the girl would be returned unharmed. After several days of captivity and deviant sexual abuse, the girl was psychologically scarred for life. Nick never forgot the vacant look in the young girl's eyes as he pursued Lavender.

Still, life with Gwyn provided the perfect buffer for the kind of dirty work Nick was required to do day after day. Even after dealing with what he called the "germs" of the world, Nick could go back to their flat at night, close the door, take his precious bride in his arms, and leave it all behind. Life was almost too good to be true.

Nick had started to feel a change come over him about that time. Before, he lived only for his work and the thrill of the chase. Now, he lived for Gwyn. Many days he found himself staring impatiently at the clock in his office, counting the minutes until he could go home. He and Gwyn were so enamored of each other, there were many nights when Nick would rush home, embrace Gwyn the moment he entered their flat, and ravage her right at the front door. Although dinner was usually ready, many nights it went untouched for hours. Gwyn proved to be as passionate and insatiable as she was beautiful. Nick had never had anyone who could make love like she could, and she'd never experienced anyone like him who could keep up with her inexhaustible appetite and creativity. They lived for each other and reveled in each other.

If only I'd gotten out while there was still time...

After six months of wedded bliss, Gwyn wanted to go to Scotland for a family visit. Nick arranged a long weekend, and they were off. When he left London, he had just cultivated a lead on the elusive Lavender, which he passed on to his partner, Gene Brodie. Lavender had been sighted in Berlin, and Brodie was going there with several other agents to bring him in. Everything looked as though it was going to go as planned, so Nick went off on his well-earned leave. Still, something in the back of his mind kept nagging at him, like the one missing word of a crossword puzzle. Something Brodie said before he left. Oh, well – there would be plenty of time to think about that when he got back.

Nick and Gwyn made the six-hour drive to Glasgow, and checked into an inn. All the way there, Nick finally started to relax for the first time in months. It helped that Gwyn couldn't keep her hands off of him, giving him a promise of what awaited him when they reached their destination.

A year and a half of intense surveillance and investigations on the Lavender business was starting to get to Nick, and he had been doing the one thing he tried so hard not to do with Gwyn – not leaving the office at the office. He never spoke of it once he got home, though, and Gwyn knew not to ask. After all, she reasoned, their time together was just that – their time. But even she could always see the wheels turning in Nick's mind, like he was trying to decipher some ancient hieroglyphic.

Even though they had planned this trip weeks before, Nick had been so busy that he forgot to visit the package store for spirits. He had planned on making this like a second honeymoon – no office, no Lavender, only the beauty of Gwyn and the Scottish Highlands for five glorious days. With her wicked sense of humor, Gwyn mockingly scolded Nick for forgetting the whiskey. Once they checked into their room, he begged forgiveness by agreeing to run down to the local pub and make reparations for his oversight.

Nick paused in his reminiscing to pour himself another glass of Scotch. He stared at the bottle in front of him through weary eyes. Nick placed his elbow on the table, rested his cheek in his open palm and closed his eyes at the memory he was recalling. After a few moments he sat back in his chair and sipped his drink.

If only I'd stayed in the room...

Nick was in the pub, purchasing two bottles of Grouse and haggling with the barkeep for some ice when he heard an explosion. Not knowing what it was, he instinctively ran into the street, along with dozens of others, only to see fire and smoke bellowing forth from the room on the 2nd floor of the inn – his room!

By the time he fought his way in, the room was totally engulfed in flame. The fire department extinguished the blaze, but Gwyn was gone.

The local police, Scotland Yard and Interpol all wrote off the explosion to a local radical arm of the IRA, but

Nick knew better. Only his room had been targeted, and his own agency later discovered that a bomb had been wired to the phone. The desk clerk remembered putting a call through to the room just before the explosion.

He had been getting too close to Lavender, putting too much pressure on him, and this had been a warning.

As Nick stood at Gwyn's grave site in Glasgow, he stared blankly at the flower-bedecked coffin. His mind wasn't idle, though. He had a rage burning deep inside. Now he was even more determined to find the man responsible for taking away the most precious gift he had ever received.

Don't worry, babe, he thought. *I'll find him. And when I do, I'll kill the son of a bitch. Here today, dead tomorrow.*

After the funeral, Nick was offered an assignment back in the U.S., but he insisted on staying in Europe. He had a job to do: find Lavender.

Nick became completely engulfed in his pursuit. The information that Lavender had been seen in Berlin turned out to be phony, but there were other leads to followup on. Nick's search took him from England to Holland, then to Portugal, then Spain, then France, and back to England. Nick grew increasingly frustrated at his inability to hit the moving target. Finding Lavender had become his life's quest. It had also become his obsession.

Nick familiarized himself even more with every detail of Miles Lavender. Every waking moment was spent reviewing, over and over again, the terrorist's traits and quirks. Nick used his analytical mind to get inside Lavender's skin, to think like he did, and tried to predict the criminal's next moves before he made them. At one point, Nick began to fear that he was getting too familiar with his prey, as he unconsciously found himself adopting some of Lavender's traits. He rationalized it, though, knowing that the best way to beat the enemy was to think and act like them. Unfortunately for those around him, one of the habits he found himself picking up was Lavender's hair-trigger temper, which caused some of his fellow team members to voice concerns about Nick's sudden short fuse and explosive outbursts.

He also started feeling that he was no better than the deviant criminal he was pursuing. Nick cynically began to think of himself as nothing more than a paid assassin. To his mind, the only difference between Nick Seven and Miles Lavender was that Nick carried a badge and had the blessing of the United States government to kill in the line of duty. The fact that Lavender was paid more for his crimes didn't help ease Nick's conscience.

Finally, Team Seven got the break it had been waiting for. An IRA informant told the agency that Lavender, along with three confederates, was indeed in London, having taken refuge in a store in the Soho area. Nick and Brodie pulled together six other members of their team, coordinated the raid with the British Secret Service and Scotland Yard, and set off to bring Lavender in. No one bothered to specify "dead or alive."

With the precision that only years of training and experience can bring, Brodie led the team through the front door of the market that was being used as the hideout. The three co-conspirators were found and taken into custody, but there was no sign of Lavender. Or of

Nick Seven.

Nick had planned this particular raid very carefully. In a private interrogation session with the informant (who really didn't miss the use of his left hand), Nick had learned that the store had a secret exit in the rear of the building, which opened into an alley. As the other agents and police were busting in the front door, Nick was in the alley behind the store, waiting. Just waiting.

Soon, his wait was over. A section of the wall slowly creaked opened, and a man cautiously exited the building. Miles Lavender. All 5 foot 6 inches of him.

Funny, Nick thought, *I always imagined he'd be taller in person.*

He waited until the man was completely out of the building. Lavender stepped into the alley, looked around, satisfied himself that he had made a successful escape, and started walking away. Nick stepped out from behind a pile of packing crates in the alley, his gun in his hand.

"Lavender," he called out. "CIA. You're under arrest. Stop and put your hands up."

Lavender stopped, and slowly turned towards Nick, who was barely visible in his black leather jacket. The light from a nearby streetlamp glinted off the barrel of Nick's gun, and some stray light also picked up the shine from Lavender's gold tooth as he smiled. Nick caught the devious smile on Lavender's face. He also had a quick mental flashback of the explosion that had killed Gwyn, and remembered once more the face of the twelve-year-old girl Lavender had tortured.

Lavender sized up his competition, and made a serious mistake: he suddenly withdrew his hand from his coat pocket, showing his hand wrapped around a Glock semi-automatic pistol, and took aim at Nick. Lavender laughed gleefully. It was the last sound he would ever make.

Nick quickly squeezed off two shots from his .357 Magnum. The first one struck Lavender in the upper left chest; the second found a home in his mid-section, and he fell on the cobblestones in a heap. Nick slowly approached the body, kicked the Glock away from Lavender's open hand, pointed the gun at him, and said "This one's for Gwyn." Then he fired a third shot between Lavender's eyes.

He was standing over the lifeless remains of the terrorist, his smoking gun still in his hand pointed at the body, almost numb, when Brodie ran into the alley.

"I think I got him, Gene," Nick managed to say.

Brodie looked at what was left of Lavender.

"I think you got him and a half," he said.

After Lavender's demise, Nick felt a void in his life. He had been so all-consumed with finding and eliminating the terrorist, that now he felt like there were no more challenges, no more hurdles to overcome. That was when he requested a transfer back to the United States and took an instructor's position at the Agency's training academy. Nick wanted to put as much distance between himself and England as possible, since there was nothing left there for him but painful memories. The only thing he missed were a couple of his friends and one of his co-workers who had been especially kind to him after Gwyn's death. But the transfer to Quantico didn't help ease the pain Nick felt, so after a year of taking raw recruits and molding them into seasoned agents, he decided to walk away and start all over again.

Nick was back in the present now. All of this reminiscing had taken him through half a bottle of Grouse and too many cigarettes.

What if I really did kill the wrong man? That means I still owe Gwyn for letting her down the way I did. I should never have left that room. If only I'd been there, if only I'd sent her out, it would have been me who answered the phone, not her. If only I'd been more careful.

Nick looked again at the gold lighter, wiped a tear from his eye, and got up from the table. Going to the bar, he picked up the phone.

"Information? Get me the number for the Holiday Inn, please."

- *Three* -

Nick and Brodie were ushered into Daniel Currey's office. Nick took a look at the trappings, noting the state-of-the-art computer system, security devices and bullet-proof glass windows, then understood why his taxes were so high.

Currey stood up as the soundproof door closed, and came out from behind his desk, extending his hand to Nick.

"Nice to see you again, Nick," he said, smiling benevolently.

Nick shook hands with his former boss, sizing him up in one quick glance. "The Old Man," as they used to call him, hadn't aged gracefully. Too many years of playing the political field, lobbying the money merchants in Washington for a few dollars more, and attending cocktail parties had taken their toll. Nick wondered why Currey, who certainly had enough years in the service to retire, kept hanging on. Passion for his work? Greed? Another challenge to overcome, like proving to the younger men that he could still cut it at his age? Or just plain stupid? Nick decided it had to be the latter.

All three men sat down, and Currey started the meeting.

"Well, Nick," he began, "I suppose Gene's given you

the rundown. This one's really got us in a box. What's your take on it?"

"I've read the reports," Nick said, "and the pattern of attacks could be the work of several groups, from the Aryan Nation to a bunch of out of control militia men holed up in some mountain in Tennessee. Why do you think it's Miles Lavender?"

"Several things," Currey answered. "One, the targets so far have appeared random, yet key. There was the bombing of a Federal Building in Cleveland, an attack on a Parochial school bus outside Chicago, a riot at a Klan rally in Birmingham where seven people were killed that was supposed to look spontaneous, and an attempted robbery of a Federal Reserve Depository in New York. That last one was unsuccessful, because one of the gang was killed trying to escape. He had the usual m.o. – no identification, no labels in his clothing, virtually untraceable – except for this."

Currey opened the lap drawer of his desk, withdrew a small item, and tossed it across the desk to Nick.

"The one we caught was carrying that," Currey said. "Look familiar?"

Nick looked at the item carefully. It was a small polished stone, a "worry stone," purple in hue, with a gold eyelet.

"What color would you say that is, Nick?" Currey asked. "A shade of lavender, isn't it? Didn't all of Miles Lavender's men carry one of those?"

"Doesn't mean anything," Nick said, setting the stone on the desk.

"All right," Currey continued, "how about this? The

man also had an L-shaped scar on his inner right forearm. If memory serves, Lavender made all of his people take a blood oath of some kind, a sort of initiation rite. Wasn't that how you were able to identify any of his band when you caught up with them?"

Nick thought for a moment.

"Could be coincidence, or a gang sign," he finally said.

"Then try this one," Currey said, leaning forward. "For the first time in over five years, Bernardi has surfaced in New York, and we think he's back in the business of dealing weapons wholesale. Wasn't he Lavender's favorite supplier, because he was loyal and wouldn't talk, no matter how much pressure we put on him?"

"Maybe Bernardi found himself a new sugar daddy," Nick finally responded.

"We don't think so," Currey said. "Bernardi had been staying very low for a long time, selling the occasional Uzi or Glock out of the trunk of his car, mostly to the mob or street punks. Now, over the last few months, Intelligence reports that he's been buying up large quantities of explosives, detonators, mercury caps, every type of weapon available – and none of it has surfaced yet."

"How do you tie all of this into Bernardi or Lavender, if the merchandise hasn't turned up?" Nick asked.

"Too many coincidences," Brodie interjected. "Nick, the attacks we've outlined so far have all of Lavender's earmarks – seemingly random targets, hundreds of miles apart so they'd look random, but all chosen to elicit the biggest outrage and response. Attacking a school bus full of Catholic schoolchildren, inciting a race riot in the

South, blowing up a Federal Courthouse where a Nazi war criminal was on trial – and that Depository in New York was no chance bank robbery that went bad. On that particular day, a shipment of gold bars was in the vaults, waiting to be transferred to Fort Knox. Do you remember the Heidelberg incident?"

Nick searched his memory for a moment, then nodded his head slowly.

"The largest diamond wholesaler in that part of Germany was robbed by five men, all wearing black ski masks and black jumpsuits, carrying Uzi's," Nick said. "One of them dropped one of those lavender worry stones on his way out. They made off with over a million dollars worth of ice, and we traced most of it to an arms dealer in Brussels, who confessed that he took it as payment for guns, ammunition and fake passports to get the men out of the country."

Currey began tapping his pencil on the desk.

"Nick," he intoned, "the men who tried to rob that Depository were dressed the same as the men who held up that diamond wholesaler in Heidelberg, and they all carried the same types of weapons as before."

Nick sat and thought for a moment, taking it all in. The wheels were turning faster than usual. Nick's mind was busy calculating the odds that his former nemesis could actually be alive. If he was, who did he kill in that alley in London five years ago? He had to find out.

"Just to be sure," Nick said slowly, choosing the words carefully, "why not exhume the body from the cemetery outside London and make sure it isn't Lavender?"

Now it was Brodie and Currey's turn to pause.

"We did, Nick," Brodie said at length. "We opened the grave, and looked inside that casket. Nick."

Seven looked at him, as Brodie's eyes bored deep into his.

"It was empty."

Nick could feel the hairs on the back of his neck stand at attention and a chill ran down his spine. All three men sat in silence for what seemed like an eternity. Finally, Nick spoke.

"I'll need backup," he said. "Three good people, no more. One of them has to be a computer and electronics expert, because things have changed since I was in the field. The other two have to be experts at handling weapons, and have no qualms about using them. Is any of my old team left?"

"You mean besides me?" Brodie asked with a slight grin.

"How long since you've been out of this office, Gene?" Nick asked.

"Not that long that I still can't match you shot for shot when it counts," Brodie answered.

"I can get you the best we have in the electronics end," Currey said. "Besides, Gene, how would you like to have Felicia back on your team?"

"Felicia?" Nick said. "I thought she went back to Barbados."

"She did," Currey answered, "but we know where she is, and we've already had contact with her. She says if you're in, she's in."

"Pretty sure of yourself, weren't you?" Nick asked rhetorically. "But if this really is Lavender, and the stakes are higher now, I don't know how safe this would be for her."

"What's wrong, Nick?" Currey challenged. "Afraid of having another dead woman on your conscience?"

Nick glared at him in silence.

"Don't kid yourself," Currey continued. "She could handle herself then, and she can handle herself even better now."

"Why, what's she been doing?" Nick asked.

Currey chuckled softly.

"Working as a bouncer in a waterfront saloon," he replied.

The next morning, Nick prepared to meet with the reactivated Team Seven in the conference room. Felicia Hagens had arrived from Barbados, and the minute Nick saw her, he removed all doubts about her fitness for the assignment – she hadn't changed in five years. She had obviously remembered her Marine training, had kept herself in shape, and still looked like she could demolish the conference table with one well-placed kick.

The newest member was a 28-year-old agent named Brad Sanders. Nick had studied his resume carefully – top 5% of his class at Dartmouth, he had been with The Agency for four years, buried in the computer and surveillance division. Nick had some initial qualms about Sanders, since he had no actual field experience, but based on his expertise he had decided to take a chance on him anyway. It was rumored that Sanders even had a bug in Currey's office, and Nick made a mental note to ask to listen to those tapes someday.

Nick stood at the front of the conference table and

looked at his team. He took a deep breath and slowly exhaled while looking each person in the eye.

"First of all," he began, "I want to thank all of you for accepting this assignment. This is going to be a tough one, and I know a few of us have been out of action for a while. Three of us have dealt with Miles Lavender before, and know full well what he's capable of."

He looked at Sanders.

"Brad," he said, "I realize this is new territory for you, being in the field. We'll help you anyway we can."

"Thanks, Mr. Seven," Sanders replied.

"Nick will do just fine," he replied with a small smile.

"You really think Lavender's still alive?" Felicia asked.

"I don't know," Nick answered. "That's what we have to find out."

He raised his coffee cup in a toast.

"Here's to the success of Team Seven," he said. "Let's start by looking at what's happened so far, and where we need to go from here."

Nick approached an erasable board on the wall of the conference room where he had written down the events that had occurred to date.

"As you can see," he began, "the first reports from the New York office outlining Bernardi's weapons trading activity were dated five weeks ago. Two weeks later was when the school bus was attacked in Chicago. One week after that the Klan rally in Alabama was disrupted. Less than a week later there was the botched robbery of the Federal Reserve in New York. And last week there was the courthouse bombing in Cleveland."

"Besides that stone they found on the guy in New

York, why you think this is Lavender?" Felicia asked in her West Indies accent.

"Think about it," Nick replied. "What were Lavender's favorite targets?"

Felicia thought for a moment before responding.

"Government buildings, Catholic churches, and anythin' else that would grab headlines," she answered.

"On the money," Nick responded. "And for the record, I'm still not convinced it's Lavender. Gene, let's see those tapes."

Brodie announced that they would be watching news tapes of the most recent attacks. Nick sat in the back of the darkened room, drinking black coffee and smoking a cigarette. Although this was a government building, and supposed to be smoke-free, Nick gave his usual response the first time someone told him to put out his cigarette, and no more was said. The four agents watched the images flashing across the wide screen television, things that would horrify the average viewer, but didn't even faze most of them – carnage, people screaming in fear, crying children being taken away by ambulances.

They had gotten up to the bombing of the Federal Courthouse in Cleveland, when something caught Nick's eye.

"Stop the tape!" he called from the back of the room.

Brodie immediately froze the image on the screen as Nick approached the front of the room.

"Rewind it," he said.

Brodie rewound the tape a few frames, until Nick told him to stop and advance it slowly. The scene was outside the courthouse, as gawking bystanders were milling about, satisfying their natural bloodlust at this tragedy. Nick watched the screen intently, until he saw what he was looking for.

"There!" he exclaimed.

Brodie stopped the tape as Nick got closer to the screen. He peered at a lone figure that was turning away from the courthouse, walking back into the crowd.

"Son of a bitch," Nick finally said in disbelief. "It's him. A little older, a little heavier, but it's him. Brad, take this section of tape, enlarge it, and get me a picture of this man."

Sanders removed the tape and took it to another room. Fifteen minutes later he returned with a photograph of the figure Nick saw. He took a long, hard look at the picture and couldn't believe what he was seeing: a ghost. It looked like Lavender, right down to the gold tooth. A dozen images from Nick's past quickly flashed through his mind, like a film being shown in fast-forward mode.

"Now I'm convinced," he said softly. "Gene, who shot this tape?"

"This came from a local news crew that was covering the trial when the explosion occurred."

"Then that's where we'll start," Nick said. "I'm going to Cleveland. Felicia, I want you to come with me. Gene, you and Brad to go to New York. Find Bernardi, lean on him, see how much he knows."

- *Four* -

It was Fall in Cleveland, and the air coming in off Lake Erie had a sharp edge to it. Nick and Felicia had reviewed Lavender's habits (although Nick still remembered them by heart), and decided to start their search in one of the older neighborhoods on the East side of the city. This was where a lot of Europeans had settled, including many from Great Britain. Nick recalled that Lavender liked the feel of home, and always sought out pubs or restaurants that would give him a little taste of England.

The first bar they went into was close to the shipyards (or what was left of them), and was a working-class establishment. Besides the low-key chatter of the working stiffs, they could hear the sound of billiards being played in the adjoining room. They had both dressed down for the occasion, trying to blend in, although the sight of a caucasian man and a dark-skinned woman with dreadlocks was a little out of place in this area. After ordering drinks, Nick called the barmaid over to the table.

"What can I get for ya?" she asked.

"Information," Nick answered, taking Lavender's picture from his jacket pocket. "Ever see this guy in here?"

"What's in it for you?" the woman asked.

"I owe him money and I want to pay up," Nick answered.

"Look, pal," she said, "in this place, nobody knows anyone, nobody sees anyone, and nobody talks about what they don't see."

"Aw, come on," he persisted. "A sharp gal like you doesn't remember a steady customer? Maybe this will help: he always orders Pernod, straight up, with an ale chaser. Coming back to you now?"

"Just a minute," she said, and returned to the bar.

She leaned over and spoke to the bartender, who went into a backroom behind the bar.

Soon, two burly men who looked like they had been kicked out of the Longshoremen for being too rough with the cargo approached Nick's table.

"Hey, you," one of them said to Nick, nudging his shoulder with a hand the size of a rump roast. "The lady says you don't listen too good. Says she told you she don't know nothin', but you don't listen too good. You got shit for brains? Or you just need your ears cleaned out, maybe."

Nick slowly pushed his chair back and stood up, making no sudden moves. He turned to face the man. Nick sized him up, and even though the guy had four inches and thirty pounds on him, he decided it was worth the gamble. With a blur of motion, Nick grabbed the man by the lapels of his jacket, slammed him into the wall behind him, raised him six inches off the ground with his right arm, and grabbed the man's crotch with his left hand. The man gasped in surprise and fear when he realized Nick had his future in the palm of his hand.

41

"Now, was I talkin' to you?" Nick asked in a quiet voice.

The other man made the mistake of trying to come to the aid of his friend. As soon as he moved towards the two men, Felicia had jumped up from her seat, grabbed the ruffian's right arm, bent it behind his back, and forced him to the floor, securing him there with her right knee planted firmly in the small of his back.

"Don't go lookin' for trouble, man," she told him. "Unless you don't need this arm no more."

Nick resumed his conversation with the first thug.

"Now, listen good," he said calmly. "I'm looking for someone, a guy who may be a regular here. I've got business with this man, and I want to find him. Do we understand each other?"

The thug could only gasp.

"I didn't catch that," Nick said.

The man nodded his head yes.

"Good," Nick continued. "Now, if you're a good boy, I'll put you down, my friend will let your buddy keep his arm, and no harm done. Otherwise..."

Nick's voice trailed off as he tightened his death grip on the family jewels. The thug took in a sharp, quick breath and his eyes bulged even more.

"I think we have achieved communication," Nick said, as he lowered the man all the way to the floor, where he lay slumped against the wall, trying to catch his breath.

Nick stepped back, wiped his hands on his jacket, and stood next to Felicia, who had let the second man get up from the floor.

"Come on," Nick said. "We'll try some other places."

As they were leaving, he stopped and turned back to address the two thugs, who were still trying to regain their composure and dignity.

"Tell everyone we'll be back in an hour," Nick said with grin.

Nick and Felicia drove their rental car a few blocks away, further into the old neighborhood. Nick had found the address of a small market that specialized in selling imported foods. Lavender liked his English ale and tea, and could probably find them only in one of these specialty shops.

They walked into the store, which was set up like the old-fashioned corner market, the kind that got run out of business by the superstores. They approached the counter, where an older woman was working. Nick showed her Lavender's picture.

"Have you seen this man in here?" he asked the woman. "He usually buys Earl Grey tea, Guinness Stout Ale and Kingsbury biscuits. Maybe Shepherd's Pie and salad cream, too."

The woman took a long hard look at the picture.

"He looks familiar, he does," she said with a British accent. "But I can't say for sure. Maybe he's been in, but not recently."

"Are there any other markets in the area that carry those items?" Nick asked.

The woman slowly shook her head 'no.'

"Not anymore," she replied. "We're the only one in this part of town."

Nick thanked her, and they left. It was getting dark, and as they drove along Superior Avenue, Nick was silent, thinking of their next move. He decided that dinner was in order, and Felicia agreed. They drove down to The Flats, a former waterfront area that now bustled with restaurants and bars. Maybe a break from the pursuit would clear his mind.

The Flats was in full happy hour mode, as men and women in business suits packed the bars. They finally found space in Sammy's, and ordered drinks – bourbon and ginger for Nick, rum and Coke for Felicia. Nick took out a cigarette, tapped the butt end a couple of times on his gold lighter and lit it, then sipped his drink.

"You oughta quit those, you know," Felicia said.

Nick chuckled softly. He looked at Felicia for a moment, a smile on his face.

"Still care about me, don't you?"

Felicia paused for a moment before answering, returning his gaze and expression. She unconsciously pushed her long woven hair back from her face with her fingers.

"I never stopped," she finally said.

"To tell the truth," Nick answered, "I never really did, either."

"So how come you never write to me all that time I'm back in Barbados?" she challenged.

"Nothing to say, I guess."

"Not even a card at Christmas. I thought about you lots the last few years, wondered how you were, what you were doin'."

"Ya know," Nick stated, "Barbados isn't really that far from the Keys. You could have hopped a boat or plane and come up yourself if you were that worried."

Felicia paused for a moment.

"No guts," she finally said.

"You? No guts? The woman who almost single-handedly took on the PLO?"

"Maybe I was afraid you wouldn't want to see me."

Nick pondered that statement for moment. He looked at Felicia across the table, and appreciated anew her South Seas beauty – smooth caramel complexion, woven hair that hung down past her shoulders, and the deepest, most sensual brown eyes he'd ever seen. The fact that she was built like a model out of Sports Illustrated (the swimsuit edition) didn't hurt, either. He had always liked and respected Felicia, and at one time had a crush on her. He even toyed with the idea of being with her when he decided to leave the business. Something he probably picked up in an old movie about running away to paradise, or some such bullshit. At the time, though, he had convinced himself that no one could ever take the place of Gwyn in his heart, and he never pursued it further, attributing his crush to rebound from having lost his wife. But that was five years ago, and this was now.

"Not a chance," he finally answered. "And you're right – I should have written, or called, or caught a plane myself. Maybe I was short on guts, too. You know, I never forgot all the kindness and compassion you showed me after Gwyn was killed. You really made it easier for me to get on with my life."

Felicia looked down in embarrassment, smiled, and let out a small laugh.

"So what's it like on Key Largo?" she asked, changing the subject.

Nick sat back in his chair, propped his right leg on his left and wistfully pondered her question.

"Gorgeous," he finally replied. "Great temperatures year 'round, bright blue water, all the fresh seafood you can handle, and the most beautiful sunsets in the world."

Felicia caught the far away look in Nick's eyes as he was fondly describing his dream come true.

"What you do for action down there?" she asked.

"I have a yacht club on the gulf," he replied.

"You like it?"

"Yeah. I really do."

"Can't be as excitin' as this," she challenged.

Nick took a puff on his cigarette before responding.

"I had enough excitement in my previous life, thank you very much," he politely replied.

Felicia looked down and smiled shyly again.

"So what we do now – tell war stories about the good old days?" she asked.

Nick shook his head.

"How about dinner, followed by a nightcap at the hotel?" he suggested.

"How about room service in your hotel suite?" she teased, her eyes twinkling.

* * *

Brodie and Sanders had wasted no time finding Bernardi in New York. The local office had kept track of him, and knew where he was at all times. They found him in a gin mill in the Bronx.

The two men approached the bar, where Bernardi was

sitting alone, nursing a beer. He was slight but wiry, with salt and pepper hair. Brodie knew that the gun merchant never went anywhere unarmed, and also knew that he kept his piece tucked under his left arm. Brodie took a stool on the left side of him, and Sanders took the one on the right. They said nothing to the old man, who was gazing intently at the bartop. Finally, Brodie leaned in close and spoke.

"Hello, Bernardi."

Bernardi looked up in surprise, startled to see his former adversary on his home turf. Bernardi quickly stuck his right hand under his coat, but it was too late. Brodie had already taken possession of his .357 Magnum.

"Now, Bernardi," he continued. "Is that any way to greet an old friend?"

"What you want, Brodie?" he stammered, obviously unnerved. "I got nothin' for you. Geez, anybody sees me hangin' wit' you, I'm dead meat."

"Then tell me what I want to know, and we'll leave."

"What?"

"Have you seen Miles Lavender lately?"

"Lavender? He's dead."

Brodie put his right arm around Bernardi's shoulder, and put his mouth near the man's ear.

"Perhaps I didn't express myself clearly enough," Brodie said softly. "I said, have you seen Lavender?"

"And I told you, Lavender's dead!"

"Then who are you buying all those weapons for – the Boy Scouts?" Brodie asked.

"Piss off, Brodie!"

Brodie tightened his grip on Bernardi's shoulder, and stood up from his stool, bringing Bernardi to his feet.

"Brad, would you excuse us for a minute? Mr. Bernardi would rather talk to me in confidence," Brodie said, dragging Bernardi towards the nearby men's room. "Let's step into your private office, where we won't be disturbed."

Sanders stayed seated at the bar, and heard what sounded like a few well-placed punches followed by muffled gasps of pain. After five minutes, Brodie came out of the men's room, alone.

"Come on," he said.

"He tell you anything?" Sanders asked.

"Enough to know that he's not supplying the Boy Scouts," answered Brodie.

The two men drove to an address on 110th street. It was an old brownstone, once stately and elegant, now merely rundown, one of those houses that was originally built for one family, but now subdivided into several low-rent apartments. Garbage cans overflowed on the sidewalk in front of the building. Brodie was thankful that it wasn't summer.

"Don't touch anything," Brodie warned Sanders as they walked into the building.

They went to apartment #2. Brodie leaned close to the door to hear if anyone was inside. After a moment he stood back, drew his Glock from his holster, and knocked on the door. Sanders, following the elder agent's lead, also took out his gun.

"Yeah?" said a man's voice from inside the apartment.

"Con Edison," Brodie said. "Checking for a gas leak."

The door opened slowly. Brodie threw himself at the door, forcing it open, and charged into the apartment, with

Sanders on his heels.

The man who opened the door was now sitting on the floor, eyes wide with fear at the sight of Brodie's gun pointed at his head.

"Your name McTavish?" Brodie asked.

"Maybe," the man replied, not knowing what to think or say.

"Maybe isn't good enough," Brodie replied. "Yes or no?"

"Yeah," the man said. "I'm McTavish. But I got no beef with you."

"Friend of yours says different," Brodie continued. "Friend of yours says you got some information I want."

"Man, I got lots of friends," McTavish said. "You gotta do better than that."

"This friend's name is Bernardi," Brodie went on. "Says he's been selling you a lot of guns and explosives. He tells me you've been buying them for someone else. He also says you've been marking up the merchandise and keeping the profits for yourself. Well?"

"Well, what?" McTavish asked.

"Well," said Brodie, "you gonna tell me who you're fronting for?"

"Ain't nobody but me," McTavish asserted. "I'm in business for myself. I'm what you call an entrepreneur."

Brodie moved the gun within two inches of McTavish's head and snapped back the latch on top of the gun, forcing a bullet from the cartridge into the chamber.

"You're gonna be a dead entrepreneur if I don't get what I want."

McTavish thought for moment. Small beads of sweat

began forming on his forehead and his heart started pounding.

"OK," he finally said, "but not here. Come in the other room, and I'll tell you."

Brodie stood back and let McTavish get up. They started walking towards the bedroom. Sanders began to follow the two men, but Brodie stopped him.

"You stay here and cover the door in case he gets company," he said.

"What if someone comes in?" asked Sanders.

"Show 'em your badge and tell 'em to have a seat," Brodie quipped.

Brodie followed McTavish into the bedroom, and the door closed behind them. Sanders waited in the living room, and couldn't help noticing the squalid furnishings. This stuff wasn't even good enough to be called second hand. He wondered why someone making money selling arms to international terrorists couldn't afford better digs.

Sanders was startled by the sound of a muffled gunshot coming from the bedroom. He charged into the room, and saw McTavish lying on the floor, a gun in his right hand, the front of his shirt discolored by a wide patch of blood. Brodie was standing a few feet away from him, his gun still in his right hand, a slight trace of smoke pouring forth from the silencer on the end.

"He went for his gun," Brodie explained. "I had no choice."

"Did you get anything from him?" asked Sanders.

"Yeah," Brodie said. "He said he was working for Lavender."

"Do you think he was telling the truth?"

Brodie held out his left hand. In the palm was one of the oval-shaped lavender stones.

"He had this in his pocket," Brodie said.

- *Five* -

It was 1:00 a.m., and Nick Seven was sitting in a chair in the living room of his suite at the Sheraton. The lights were off and he was nursing a glass of Scotch (not Grouse, but the best the hotel had in the bar). He took an occasional drag from his cigarette. This was another of those thinking moments for him. He replayed the day's events in his mind, trying to decide what his next move would be. He also wondered how Brodie had fared in New York.

From the adjoining bedroom, he heard the rustle of sheets. Felicia came into the room, stark naked, and approached him.

"What you doin' up at this hour?" she asked, rubbing the sleep from her eyes.

"Couldn't sleep," Nick replied.

Felicia laughed softly, and came up behind Nick, planting a kiss on his neck.

"Guess I'm losin' my touch," she said. "After tonight, you should sleep like a baby for a week."

Nick smiled at her.

"It wasn't you," he said. "I've just got too much on my mind."

Felicia began massaging the back of his neck.

"Man, you tight as a bedspring," she said. "You never learned how to relax, that's your trouble. Put yourself in my hands. Felicia teach you how to unwind."

Nick closed his eyes and found himself enjoying her touch. He had forgotten how nice it was to have this kind of attention from someone who really cared about him. Maybe he had been alone too long, after all. Felicia stopped rubbing his neck and pulled up a chair.

"You got another glass?" she asked, pointing to the bottle of Scotch.

"You gonna put on some clothes?" he responded, with a trace of mock annoyance.

"Whatsa matter – tough guy like you afraid of a naturalist?" she teased.

Nick got a glass, picked up the bottle, and started to pour her some Scotch.

"Say when," he said.

"How 'bout forever?" she coyly asked.

Nick stopped pouring, and handed her the glass.

"How about we talk about this after the job is done?" he replied.

"OK." She took the glass.

Nick took his seat, and lit another cigarette.

"When did you start drinking Scotch?" he asked in mock surprise. "I thought Rum was the national beverage of Barbados."

"Sometimes you take whatever's available," she said.

"Is that what tonight was all about?" he asked. "Was I just whatever was available?"

"No, Nick," she said. "Don't sell yourself short. I wanted this for a long time."

Nick paused a moment before responding. He gazed at Felicia in the dim light and realized how much he had missed her since he left England years earlier. Maybe he really was ready this time.

"I guess I did, too," he said.

"Then why you wait so long?" she asked.

"I don't know," he answered. "Just didn't think I was ready, but maybe now I am."

"Maybe you were afraid," Felicia said.

Nick narrowed his eyes and looked at her. Even in the dark, she looked damn good.

"Afraid of what?"

"I know you a long time, Nick. Just like Brodie. We been through a lot together. I knows you better than you knows yourself. I know how hard it was on you when your wife got killed. You think you the only one lost someone close? I know how you felt when you shot Lavender, and I know how you feel right now – you think he's still out there somewhere, and you have to kill him all over again. But you can't kill a ghost."

"You think he isn't alive and terrorizing?"

"I only know the facts. And the fact is, you killed that bastard once, and he don't come back from Hell. At least, not without help."

"But help from who?"

"That's what we got to figure out, Hon."

Nick took a sip of Scotch and another drag from his cigarette. He thought about what Felicia had said.

"Who contacted you about this assignment?" he finally asked.

"Brodie," she answered. "Why?"

"Currey led me to believe he talked to you."

"I don't speak to Currey until I come back to Langley three days ago. Hell, I got no use for that ass-kisser, and never did."

Nick sat silent for a few minutes. His mind was racing again. Something from the inner recesses of his memory was trying to speak to him, but he couldn't bring it out. Something he had buried long ago, something he didn't want to face. Something that happened right before Gwyn was killed. What was it? He was also curious about something else.

Why did Currey make me think he contacted Felicia and put the team back together? Nick thought.

Felicia set her glass down on the table, and stood up.

"I'm turnin' in," she said. "You comin'?"

"I'll be along in a few," Nick said.

Felicia bent down, kissed him on the cheek, and walked towards the bedroom.

"Hey," Nick called out. "Were you really working as a bouncer in a waterfront bar?"

Felicia stopped, turned and looked at him over her shoulder, smiled slyly and winked. Nick admired her statuesque silhouette in the dim light.

Remind me never to get her pissed off at me, he thought.

"Well, tough guy," she teased. "You comin'?"

Nick snuffed out his cigarette and approached Felicia at the doorway. Wrapping his arms around her, they began ravenously kissing each other. She gently rubbed his shoulders and back, then untied his robe, moving her hands inside to massage his naked flesh. Nick ran his hands over Felicia's smooth skin, caressing her ample breasts before moving his hands over the rest of her torso. Her perfume was like an instant aphrodisiac, turning him into an animal. Pushing him back against the doorframe, Felicia placed her arms around Nick's shoulders, hoisted herself up and wrapped her legs around his waist. Nick found himself involuntarily responding to her aggressive and passionate lovemaking. He moved his hands down to Felicia's firm buttocks and carried her to the bed, where he continued to ravage her a second time.

* * *

The next morning, Brad Sanders was sitting at the desk in his hotel room in New York, with his laptop computer, writing his report of the previous night's events. His computer was plugged into the modem in the room, so his report was going directly to headquarters via e-mail, with a copy being forwarded to Nick in Cleveland. When he had finished, he was about to hit the "send" button, but remembered something that he always did while working in the Intelligence division. Before sending the report, he inserted a floppy disc into the laptop, copied his report onto it, then sent it on. He removed the disc and placed it in his briefcase.

Brodie had left the hotel earlier, saying he was going to check with the Customs Department and the airlines to see if anyone fitting Lavender's description had recently entered or left the country.

In Cleveland, Nick received the report on his laptop, read it carefully, then sent a return e-mail to Sanders, instructing him to have Brodie call him when he returned. Nick sat back in his chair, lit a cigarette and started thinking.

OK, tough guy, he thought. *You haven't been out of the game so long that you've forgotten how to play. Let's see – if you were Miles Lavender and you'd just pulled off another job, would you hang around for more, or would you move on to the next target? What would that next target be? You've already followed your usual routine and scatter pattern. Would it be something else in the U.S., or would you go back to more familiar territory?*

Felicia entered the room, kissed Nick on the cheek and poured a cup of coffee from the room service cart.

"What's the plan for today?" she asked.

"After Brodie calls me I'm going to the TV station that sent us the news footage we saw," Nick replied. "I'll look at all the tape they shot that day. Maybe there's something they edited for broadcast that's useful."

"What do you want me to do?"

"I want you to catch a commuter to Chicago and do the same thing. Examine the tapes from that school bus attack. These events happened a couple of weeks apart, so maybe our friend did some traveling. Be back here in time for dinner."

Felicia called the airport, booked a roundtrip seat on a commuter that was leaving for Chicago at 11:00, grabbed her coat and handbag, and prepared to leave.

"See you at The Diamondback at 6:00," Nick said as she went out the door.

Back in New York, Brodie had returned to the hotel. Customs had no record of Miles Lavender entering or leaving the country recently, nor did Immigration, but that didn't surprise the veteran sleuth, as it was highly unlikely Lavender would use his real name. The airlines had been nice enough to provide a list of all passengers who had departed New York for England in the past two weeks. It was a lengthy list, containing more than three hundred names, but they would all have to be checked out.

He sat down with Sanders, and they reviewed the lists. They eliminated anyone who had booked round-trip passage, figuring they were just going to London for a long weekend or vacation. Also eliminated were those traveling as part of a tour group, and anyone over the age of 60 or under 40. That whittled the list down to an almost-manageable eighty-five names. Of those names, they checked any that were aliases previously used by Lavender, or any variation thereof, and highlighted those that matched. Brodie instructed Sanders to fax the list to the London office, with instructions to check out all the names. As he went to the hotel's concierge desk to do this, Brodie called Nick in Cleveland.

"Did you find our Uncle Mike?" Nick asked, using code words.

"Uncle Mike was here, visiting friends and relatives," Brodie responded. "One of them took sick, though, and had to see a specialist."

"Yes, I read that in the postcard you sent. How are you coming along with the rest of the family reunion?"

"Most of them are out of town, but we've sent invitations."

"Any RSVP's yet?"

"No, but give me a couple of days and we should have

some responses."

"How's the weather on the coast?"

"Cloudy, but I expect the sun to come out anytime now. How is it in Cleveland?"

"About the same. I'm going sight-seeing today. I hear there's a great movie I should see that Grandpa Dan recommended."

"Have a nice time. I'll talk to you later."

Nick hung up, grabbed his coat, and prepared to leave. Before going, he took a few things out of his suitcase that he had requisitioned from the property office before leaving Langley: a pocket camera that looked like a pager but could store up to twenty pictures as well as thirty minutes of video, and a wristwatch with a digital tape recorder built into the band. As he put the items in their respective places, he chuckled to himself, thinking how you used to have to be in the Agency to get these James Bond gadgets, but now you could get them through on-line merchants or at any local Radio Shack. How times had changed. He also put his 9mm Beretta in his shoulder holster. This had changed, too – Nick remembered when the .38 revolver or .357 Magnum was the weapon of choice among most agents.

Thirty minutes later, Nick was sitting in a room at WJW TV, watching the video tapes taken during the Courthouse bombing a week earlier. This had been a big story, and there was at least three hours worth of tape to sift through. Armed with a cup of coffee, Nick sat and watched, keenly looking for that one image that would unlock everything. Much of it was a replay of what he had seen a few days ago, but he watched it all over again anyway. The videographer on the scene had taken great pains to capture as much of the action as he could, including interviews and reactions from bystanders.

Finally, during hour number three, Nick suddenly sat upright in his chair. He grabbed the remote control, stopped the tape, and rewound it a few frames until he found the spot he wanted to replay. Advancing the tape frame by frame, Nick froze the picture when he saw what had attracted his attention. It was another of the crowd scenes, with people milling about after the bombing. He stood up, went close to the screen, and peered intently at one of the faces in the crowd.

"I don't believe it," he muttered to himself in disbelief.

He took the camera from his coat pocket, focused on the face in question, and took several pictures. Sitting back down, he decided to play the rest of the tape, to see if anything else was noteworthy. He finished viewing the tapes, found nothing significant, and returned them to the station, thanking them for doing their part for God and Country.

Once outside the studio, Nick took the cell phone from his pocket and called Felicia in Chicago. She was viewing news tapes at the studios of WGN. Nick told her what he had seen in the tapes of the Cleveland incident, and instructed her to look for the same thing. He also cautioned her not to say anything to anyone else on the team except him if she found what he thought she would. Nick returned to his hotel and paged Brad Sanders. Several minutes later, Sanders called him back.

"Are you alone?" Nick asked.

"Yeah," said Sanders. "Gene went out to check on one

of the names on the list, someone who came back to New York. Did you get my report this morning?"

"Yeah. Only one thing, you misspelled Brodie's name. It's 'i-e,' not 'y.'"

"Sorry."

"I need a favor," Nick continued. "I need to know what Currey has been talking about in his office the past couple of months."

There was an awkward silence. Finally, Sanders spoke. "What do you mean?" he asked cautiously.

"Don't worry, kid," Nick assured him. "I'm not gonna bag you for bugging the old man's office. I don't care about the how, only the what. Can you get me something?"

"I have transcripts on my discs, if that will help."

"Perfect. Now, do exactly what I tell you, and don't write this down, OK?"

"Sure," Sanders said, obviously pleased at getting to do something besides routine desk duty. He listened carefully as Nick gave him a list of detailed instructions.

"But what will I tell Gene?" Sanders asked.

"I'll take care of that. Just get busy on what I gave you, and I'll see you later. Have Gene call me here when he gets back in."

"Got it," said Sanders, and hung up.

Nick booted up his laptop, logged into the Agency database using his newly-assigned password, and accessed the files on Miles Lavender. He was looking for something, but in his heart he hoped he wouldn't find it.

He read the most recent entries, detailing everything he and Currey had talked about a few days ago – the attacks, the exhumation of Lavender's body, finding the purple-colored worry stone on the body of the would-be bank robber in New York and the Intelligence reports on Bernardi. It was all there, but Nick was looking for the one thread that connected everything.

Finally, he found it. His heart sank, and he slumped back in his chair, staring at the screen. There it was, in plain sight for anyone to see, if only they'd been looking for it. He quickly inserted a floppy disc into the computer, and downloaded the pages he needed from the file. He removed the disc and logged off. The disc went into the breast pocket of his jacket. Nick sat back, lit a cigarette and started thinking.

Now I know where you are. You followed your usual routine, just like you always did. So damned predictable, and still dealing from the bottom of the deck.

Nick was jolted back to reality by the ringing of the telephone. It was Brodie.

"Yeah, Nick," Brodie began. "What's up?"

"I think I found something. It looks like our friend took a trip back home. I need you to get to London and start checking the old hideouts and contacts. While you're there, you can follow-up personally on that list you sent off this morning. I still have one or two more things to check on this end, so I'll meet you there the day after tomorrow."

"OK," Brodie said. "Sanders and I will leave right away."

"No," Nick interjected, "I'm sending Brad back to Langley to check something from the files."

"What did you find, Nick?"

"Something I can't talk about over the phone. Just get to London and I'll fill you in personally in a day or so. We're close, Gene, real close."

"Sure, Chief," Brodie answered. "I'll catch the redeye to Heathrow."

Nick hung up and leaned back in his chair, crossing one leg over the other. He puffed his cigarette while thinking.

"Catch the redeye", he thought. *Why does that sound so familiar? Dammit, Seven, think – why can't you remember where you heard that before?*

- *Six* -

Diamondback's was busy with the dinner crowd. Nick had a table for two on the enclosed deck outside, where you could command a view of Lake Erie, and of the marinas. Looking at the yachts and pleasure craft docked there made him feel a little homesick for the peaceful world he had left on the Keys only days earlier. Soon, he told himself, very soon he'd be back there.

Felicia came into the restaurant, spied Nick, and sat down at the table. After ordering drinks, she relayed what she had found in Chicago.

"You were right, Hon. I watched all the tapes, and found what you were lookin' for. I got it on film. Here."

She started to reach into her handbag, but Nick held up his hand. "Give it to me back at the hotel," he said.

"So what we do now?" she asked.

"Order dinner," Nick answered. "This place is supposed to serve a killer salmon steak."

"Man, how can you think about eatin' with what we found out today?" she asked incredulously. "You got to do somethin' 'bout this!"

"I already have," Nick assured her. "Good things come to those who wait – or have you forgotten about last night already?"

"No, I haven't forgotten," she said, still slightly miffed at what she perceived as Nick's reluctance to take immediate action of some sort.

Nick reached into his jacket pocket, withdrew a white envelope, and slid it across the table to Felicia.

"What's this?" she asked, picking it up.

"Open it," Nick answered.

She opened the envelope, and found a plane ticket, and a key.

"That plane leaves Hopkins Airport tomorrow morning at 11:00," Nick said. "Non-stop to Miami. The key is to my condo on Key Largo, and the address is in there. I want you to go there, watch your back, and wait for me."

"I don't get it," she said, with a cross between confusion and anger. "You sendin' me away?"

"Yes," Nick said, "I am. It's going to get ugly over the next couple of days, and I don't want you in the line of fire."

Felicia slammed the envelope down on the table.

"Now, you listen to me, Nick Seven," she scolded. "I can take care of myself. Been doin' it for a long time, and I don't need no man to tell me different!"

Nick looked at her for a moment before he spoke. Finally, he leaned closer to the table, and spoke softly, yet intently.

"Now, you listen," he began, placing his hand on hers as he spoke. "I have a job to do, some old business to finish so we can get on with our life. I don't want any ghosts rattling around in our closet. I've already lost one woman I cared about, and I'm not going double or nothing. Understand?"

Felicia was about to speak, when she realized something Nick had said.

"OUR life?" she asked.

Nick slowly nodded his head.

"That's right – ours," he said. "I want you to go to Key Largo and wait for me – and be there with me."

She looked down at the envelope, unconsciously rearranged her hair with her fingers and gave that shy little-girl smile that Nick found so captivating. Looking up, she said, "Forever?"

"The job isn't finished yet," Nick said with a small smile.

Felicia took the envelope and put it in her purse.

"OK, tough guy," she said. "You win – this time."

Later that night, Nick was sitting in his hotel suite. He had taken the digital camera that Felicia had used in Chicago earlier that day and was downloading the images through his laptop computer. He had to be sure that what she saw matched what he found in his viewing of the news video tape in Cleveland. After a few minutes, an image appeared on the screen. Nick looked at the face before him for a few minutes, then leaned back in his chair. Crossing one leg over the other, he lit a cigarette and took a sip of Scotch while continuing to stare, somewhat in disbelief, at the screen.

So you were in Chicago, too, he thought. *You just had to be there to see your handiwork carried out, didn't you? Just like you did in Cleveland, and everywhere else. You haven't changed. Now I know what I have to do – again. This time, though, I'll do it right.*

Nick arrived in Toronto, Canada the next afternoon. He

had not told Brodie or Felicia that he was coming here en route to London. Some things you just had to keep to yourself.

His cab dropped him off at the front entrance of the Landau Hotel. Nick handled the usual business with the cabbie, then went inside. All the way from the airport, he had the feeling that he wasn't alone, and he was about to prove it. Nick approached the counter of the gift shop.

"Can I help you, sir?" the man behind the counter asked.

"Yes," Nick said. "Do you have any American cigarettes?"

"What brand would you like, sir?" the man asked.

"Winston, please," Nick replied.

The man slid a pack of Winston's across the counter.

"I prefer them in a box, if you have them," Nick said.

"Of course, sir," the man said, as he went to a rack of cigarettes towards the back of the counter area.

Nick hoped the balding man pretending to read the newspaper ten feet away was catching all of this. The clerk returned with Nick's cigarettes, and rang up his purchase. Nick tucked the cigarettes into his pocket and started to walk away.

"Oh, sir!" the clerk called out. "You forgot your matches."

Nick returned to the counter and accepted the book of matches the man handed him, with the hotel's logo on the cover. Nick stepped outside, took a cigarette out of the pack, and lit it with one of the matches.

"Pardon me, chap," someone said. "Have you a light?"

Nick turned and came face to face with the man who

had been following him.

"Sure," Nick said, handing him the book of matches.

The man lit his cigarette, thanked Nick, and started to walk away.

"Just a minute," Nick called after him. "Can I have my matches back, please?"

"Oh, of course," the man said, reaching into his pocket and handing Nick a book of matches. "Dreadfully sorry."

The man continued on down the street at a rapid pace. Nick looked at the book of matches – same logo as the one he had gotten inside, but when he opened the book, he saw that half of the matches were gone. Nick chuckled softly and hoped the man would have fun waiting at the bogus address that was written inside the other book of matches.

Nick went back into the hotel and took the elevator to the 15th floor. He went to room 1504, and knocked.

"Who is it?" said a voice from inside.

"Snow White," Nick answered.

The door was opened by Brad Sanders, who let Nick in, locking the door behind him.

"Did you have any trouble?" Nick asked.

"No," answered Sanders. "I don't think I was followed, and Brodie bought your story about sending me back to headquarters. Any trouble at the newsstand downstairs?"

"Ultra smooth," Nick answered. "You should get out into the field more often. Now, what have you got for me?"

They went to the laptop computer on the desk. Brad pulled up some files from the disc, and Nick read the transcriptions of Currey's "private" conversations. Most of it was dull political bullshit, but he did find one conversation with Gene Brodie to be of interest. Nick read the pages twice, committing the contents to memory.

"OK," he finally said. "You did good. That's what I was looking for. But I do have a question – what really happened in New York after you and Gene found Bernardi?"

"Well," Sanders began, "we drove to this address on 110th street, found the guy named McTavish, he wouldn't tell us anything while I was in the room, so he and Gene went into the bedroom, and a few minutes later I heard the gunshot. When I went in, Gene told me that McTavish pulled a piece on him, and he had to shoot him in self defense. He also showed me the purple worry stone, and said McTavish had it in his pocket."

"You didn't see Gene take it from McTavish's pocket?"

"No," Brad said, with a quizzical look on his face. "But now that you mention it, there was something else peculiar about that night that I forgot about until just now."

"What?"

"When we went into McTavish's apartment and Gene drew his gun, he didn't have a silencer on it, but when I went into the bedroom after the shooting, he did. What do you make of that?"

Nick said nothing, thinking about what Sanders had just told him.

"I want you to go back to Langley for real this time, and I'll be in touch in a couple of days," he said. "You can leave first thing in the morning. In the meantime, enjoy Toronto – they've got a helluva night life here."

"What will you be doing?" Brad asked.

"I have some things to take care of," Nick answered. "I'll stop by and get you at 7:00 in the morning. We can share a cab to the airport."

"Aren't you going back home?"

"No," Nick answered, "I have a date in London with an old friend."

Nick checked into his room at The Landau and made a phone call. Thirty minutes later, he left the hotel and hailed a taxi out front, giving the driver his destination. Fighting the rush hour traffic, the cab deposited Nick at The Montmarte Grill forty-five minutes later. He went inside and took a seat at one of the cocktail tables in the bar. After ordering a bourbon and ginger ale, he lit a cigarette and waited. Ten minutes later, his guest arrived.

"Hi, Nick," a soft voice said.

Nick looked up to see Sylvia Trench standing at the table. He instinctively rose from his seat and held a chair for the statuesque blonde. Sylvia was wearing an attractive gown that showcased her stunning beauty and smoldering looks. After ordering a Martini, she and Nick began to talk.

"Nick Seven," she began. "The last person in the world I expected to hear from. How long has it been?"

"A lifetime," Nick replied.

"I was really surprised to get your call," Sylvia said. "Is this business or pleasure?"

"Sorry to disappoint you, Sylvia, but it's business."

"I was afraid of that. What's on your mind?"

"I need the use of those light fingers of yours tonight."

Sylvia got a look of astonishment on her face.

"Whatever do you mean?" she asked in mock surprise.

"Come on, Sylvia," Nick replied. "You're the best pickpocket this side of New York City."

Sylvia stifled a laugh.

"OK," she said. "Guilty as charged. Who's the mark?"

"He'll be waiting at The French Quarter Bistro in an hour," Nick explained. "He's about five foot ten, medium build, salt and pepper hair, bald on top. When I saw him earlier he was wearing a cheap blue pinstripe suit and a gray overcoat."

"What do you want me to do when I find this guy?"

Nick paused a moment. "Get his identification and find out who he is," he replied.

"Then what?"

"Call me at The Landau. I'm in room 1206."

"What's so special about this guy?"

"He was following me this afternoon from the minute I hit town. I shook him by letting him think I was meeting someone at The French Quarter at 8:00. He'll probably have a book of matches from The Landau, too."

Sylvia slowly nodded her head.

"I can handle that," she said, pausing to lick her lips seductively. "But wouldn't it be better if I delivered the information in person?"

Nick chuckled softly, catching the come-hither look in her eyes.

"I'll have to take a raincheck," he said, reaching into his breast pocket and extracting some folded money. "But this should compensate you for your time."

Sylvia stopped his hand as he slid the money across the table.

"Save your money, Nick," she said. "Let's consider this a personal favor for old time's sake, OK?"

Nick looked at her for a second.

"OK," he finally said.

Sylvia got up from the table.

"I'll call you later," she said.

Nick had dinner while he was at The Montmarte, then went back to his hotel. He was too wound up, so he decided to take a walk through the city to relax before going up to his room. He walked several blocks to Eaton Center, and looked up at the six-story glass shopping mall. Nick continued his walk, dodging people coming out of the shopping complex. The night air had turned cold, so Nick pulled up the collar on his coat and stuffed his hands in the pockets.

Nick was about three blocks from his hotel. The sidewalk was deserted, and only the occasional car or taxi went by. He was thinking about his current case, and also found his mind wandering to Felicia, wondering if she was in Key Largo. Seeing Sylvia Trench tonight had made him think of her, and it was a strange feeling for Nick. Maybe he was changing again – in the past, he would have taken Sylvia up on her offer of a private audience in his hotel room without hesitation, but not now. He started remembering how good it had been to be with Felicia in Cleveland. Of course, he also recalled some exciting nights with Sylvia Trench, which brought a grin to his face as he walked.

Nick was so wrapped up in thought that he didn't see the person standing in the darkened alley across the street. He also didn't see the gloved hand, or the silenced gun the hand was pointing in his direction. The shooter slowly moved the gun, following Nick as he walked along the street.

Nick was passing a boutique that was closed for the evening. He didn't hear the gunshot, only the impact it made on the window six inches in front of his face. Out of reflex, Nick instantly flattened himself on the pavement, reached inside his coat, and withdrew his gun. Finding the entrance to the shop, Nick crawled in and hugged the wall, his Beretta in his right hand, ready to fire. He cautiously peered across the street in the direction the shot had come from. Another shot hit the building, missing Nick by inches, but taking out a chunk of the brownstone frame. He leaned back, trying to lose himself in the shadows.

Five minutes passed with no more gunshots. Nick peeked out from the doorway, but no one fired on him this time. After another five minutes, he decided it was safe to continue his journey. He holstered his gun and stepped out of the doorway to survey the damage. Two shots, two very near-misses. Nick knew you had to be a damn good marksman to miss that close.

An hour later, he was having a drink in his room when the phone rang. It was Sylvia Trench.

"I got what you wanted, Nick," she said. "The guy's name is Peter Lamont. He's a local private investigator. You want his address?"

"No, thanks," Nick answered. "Did you have any trouble?"

Sylvia chuckled softly. "The only trouble I had was figuring out how this guy stays in business. It was so easy to lift his wallet I almost felt sorry for him."

"That's how I felt this afternoon when it was so obvious he was following me," Nick replied. "When did you leave Lamont?"

"About a half-hour ago."

"So he was with you for the past two hours?"

"Yes," Sylvia answered. "Why?"

"Someone took a couple of shots at me on the street about an hour ago," Nick replied.

"It couldn't have been Lamont. He was with me. Besides, I doubt that idiot could even hold a gun."

Nick chuckled softly to himself.

"You're probably right," he said. "Listen, Sylvia, I appreciate your help tonight. Are you sure I can't pay you for your time and trouble?"

"No need to," she answered. "Lamont took care of that for you – only he doesn't know it yet."

Nick laughed.

"You haven't changed," he said. "Thanks again, and if you're ever in Key Largo, be sure and look me up."

"It's a date," Sylvia said, hanging up.

Nick sat down at the table and sipped his drink. He took out a cigarette and tapped it on the gold lighter before lighting up. Still thinking. Someone apparently thought that what he was doing was important enough to warrant hiring a private investigator to keep tabs on him, and take two shots at him. That also meant that someone knew he had made a side trip to Toronto from Cleveland. But who?

- *Seven* -

Brad Sanders had taken Nick's advice, and gone out to sample the after hours activities this Canadian metropolis had to offer. When he got back to his room, he was too keyed up to sleep and was sitting at the computer on his desk, the radio tuned to a local jazz station, wrapped up in designing some new program he had been working on. Since he was going back to the office in the morning, he rationalized, he may as well get a head start on the work that would be waiting for him there.

He was so absorbed in his configurations and the smooth background music that he didn't hear the door to his room being jimmied open, nor the soft footsteps of the man entering his room. The figure in the black overcoat crept up silently behind Sanders, and raised a knife with his gloved right hand.

Brad Sanders felt the sharp thrust of the blade as it penetrated the middle of his back between his shoulders. As he gasped in pain and surprise, he glanced at his computer screen, and saw the reflection of his assailant. He tried to get up from his chair, but the knife had done its job, and he slumped on the desk, feeling the life draining out of him. The man who had stabbed him quickly grabbed the computer discs that Sanders had laying on the desk, put them in his overcoat pocket, then approached the baseboard and pulled the modem connection for the computer out of the database port. He calmly left the room, closing the door behind him.

Sanders was dying, but he wasn't gone yet. He had to leave a message, a clue of some kind. He reached for the phone with his right hand, and managed to pick it up from the receiver. It was one of the modern digital phones that displayed the number being called on an illuminated screen in the receiver. With all the strength he could muster, Sanders pushed some numbers – 27639.....

The receiver fell on the desktop as Brad Sanders gasped his final breath.

Nick Seven arrived at Sanders' room at 7:00 the next morning. He knocked, but when no one answered, he tried the knob, found the door ajar, and instinctively drew his gun. He slowly pushed the door open and stepped inside. Directly in front of him he saw Sanders' lifeless body slumped on the desk. Nick holstered his weapon, and approached the body of his dead teammate. The knife was still lodged in Sanders' back.

Nick shook his head slowly and sighed.

"Damn it!" he softly muttered.

Nick looked around the room, but saw no signs of a struggle. He was about to leave, when he noticed the phone near Brad's right hand. He carefully picked it up, and read the numbers that were still stored in the phone's memory chip: 27639.

That's only five numbers, Nick thought. *Who was he trying to call? If he was in trouble, why not call the front desk for help?*

Nick reset the connection on the phone, and called the local police. He then placed a call to CIA headquarters, and asked to speak with Daniel Currey.

"This is Seven," he said when Currey came on the line. "We've got a man down."

"Who?" Currey anxiously asked.

"Sanders," Nick answered.

"Where are you?"

"Toronto, Canada," Nick answered.

"What happened?" Currey demanded.

"I don't know all the details," Nick replied, "but I just came to his hotel room and he was dead. Stabbed with a knife between his shoulders. He never saw it coming."

Currey exhaled heavily.

"Dammit, Nick," he reprimanded, "you knew Sanders was new to working in the field. You were supposed to look out for him. What the hell was he doing in Toronto, anyway?"

"He was here under my orders," Nick replied. "Look, Dan, you put me in charge of this team, remember? That means you gave me full responsibility, which I take for what happened to Brad. And that's not all. Last night someone took a couple of potshots at me on the street in front of my hotel."

"You think it's Lavender?"

"Who else?" Nick asked rhetorically. "I need you to make arrangements to get Brad's body back to the States. I have to catch a plane to London in two hours."

Currey paused for a moment.

"All right," he finally said. "I'll contact our Bureau up there and tell them to make the necessary arrangements.

Which hotel is he in?"

"The Landau. Room 1504. I've already called the local cops, so tell your people up here to hurry."

"What about the Canadian Police?"

"I'll handle them," Nick said. "What's the codeword for me to give to our local people?"

"Slidepeel," Currey answered.

"Thanks," Nick said, hanging up.

The police and the agents from the Toronto field office arrived almost simultaneously. Nick gave his version of events, and explained to the Toronto cops that Sanders was a government agent working undercover. The paramedics had also arrived and took the body from the room. Nick conferred briefly with the agent from the Toronto office, who assured him that Brad Sanders would be transported back to the United States that afternoon. The local police had no reason to hold Nick, so he was able to make his plane for London.

The flight arrived at Heathrow airport on schedule, and there was a car waiting for Nick. On the ride to the Agency's London office, he set his watch back five hours to adjust to the time change from North America. While doing so, he checked to make sure the recording device hidden in the watchband was working. He also checked the clip in his Beretta to be sure it was fully loaded.

Nick stepped into the London office for the first time in over five years, and had to stop for a moment. It was like stepping back in time. After getting over the shock of being there again, he was shown to his temporary office, and provided with a cup of coffee.

"Where's Brodie?" he asked the agent in charge.

"He went out to follow up on a name from that list he sent us, sir," said the agent. "Should be back anytime. Can I get you anything else, Mr. Seven?"

"No, thank you," Nick replied.

The agent left the office, closing the door behind him. Nick picked up the phone, made a call to the Customs Department, asked a couple of questions, and hung up. He then booted up the computer on his desk to check some old files. He hoped the Agency's database still had information on file from his previous assignment in England five years earlier.

Silly question, he thought. *These people still have an open file on Hitler, for Christ's sake.*

After thirty minutes of searching, Nick found what he was looking for, and added the information to the disc he had used in Cleveland.

Nick turned his swivel chair around and looked out the window at the bustling traffic and pedestrians on the street below. He leaned back, took a sip of coffee (and remembered that you couldn't find a decent cup of coffee anywhere in the United Kingdom), lit a cigarette, and started thinking.

He was transported back in time to that fateful night five years earlier, the night he and Gwyn had taken the trip to Glasgow. It was all coming back to him now, the one thing he had been repressing for so long.

He was ready to leave that afternoon for his long-awaited trip, when Brodie had come into his office.

"Nick," he said, "we've just gotten a lead from one of our informants. It looks like Lavender is in Berlin."

"How reliable is it?" Nick asked.

"This guy's given us some pretty solid stuff before," Brodie answered. "Besides, we heard from our Berlin office that there's been a lot of weapons trading going on, as though someone's got something big planned."

"Yeah, it does," Nick said, thinking how disappointed Gwyn was going to be when he told her they'd have to cancel their trip. "OK, Gene, book two tickets to Berlin. We'll leave in the morning."

Brodie shook his head in an emphatic "no."

"Not 'we,'" he said. "You're going away, remember?"

"But Gene," Nick protested, "if this is on the level, and Lavender really is in Berlin, I want to be there when we collar him."

"Forget it," Brodie persisted. "I know that feisty bride of yours, and she'll broil my butt for dinner if I take you away from her this weekend. Besides, this is probably another dead end, and if Lavender was there, he's long gone by now. You go on your trip, and I'll catch the redeye to Berlin."

Nick began replaying the rest of that night in his mind – the walk to the pub for the Scotch and ice; the explosion; the fire. Funny, he never thought about it until now, but there was one thing that was out of place about that night. He also knew why he hadn't remembered it. Nick had made such a concentrated effort to put it all behind him and get on with his life that he didn't really want to see the obvious. Maybe he'd been in a state of denial all these years. That was about to change. Nick knew where his elusive moving target was, and now it was time to take care of some old business – again.

His train of thought was interrupted by a knock on the

office door. The door opened, and Gene Brodie came in. He approached Nick and they shook hands.

"Howdy, partner," Brodie said. "When did you get in?"

"About an hour ago," Nick answered.

"Did you get everything tied up in Cleveland?"

"Yeah. How have you made out over here?"

Brodie shook his head in disgust.

"We checked every name on that passenger list, and none of them fits the bill," he said. "But didn't you say you knew Lavender was here?"

Nick narrowed his eyes and looked at his partner.

"Yeah," he finally said. "Our friend is definitely in London. Come on. Let's take a ride."

It was getting dark, and the Fall night had a chill in the air. Nick had signed out a car, and he and Brodie drove to the Soho area. They chatted on the way, about nothing in particular, mostly small talk. Finally, they arrived at a small market, which was closed.

"Hey," said Brodie, "isn't this the place we found Lavender before?"

"Yeah," said Nick.

"You really think he's dumb enough to come back here after all these years?"

"Why not?" Nick answered. "If he thinks he's safe by us believing he's dead, what has he got to lose? He thinks he's as free as a bird, with no cats after him. Come on, let's go around back to that secret doorway."

The two men left the car, and walked around to the back of the building. The cobblestoned alley hadn't changed in five years – still lined with packing crates and garbage cans, and still illuminated by that lone streetlamp.

Nick took a deep breath, exhaled, and walked into the alley. It isn't often a man gets to replay a significant part of his past, to get a second chance to do it right, but this was going to be tougher than he thought.

"Check that section of the wall about ten feet right of the door," Nick said. "That's the part that opens from the inside, the one Lavender used to escape the first time."

Brodie examined the part of the building in question, but could find no way to open the hidden passageway.

"No good," he finally said. "We'll never get in this way. I don't think our man is here, Nick."

"Yes, he is," said Nick.

Brodie turned around, only to see Nick pointing his gun at him.

"What's this?" Brodie asked quizzically. "A gag?"

"No gag, Gene," Nick said. "Only a question: why?"

"Why what?" Brodie asked in response.

"Why fake the resurrection of Miles Lavender? Why all those pseudo-terrorist attacks in the U.S.? Why bring me back into the game?" He stopped for a moment, his voice getting an angry edge to it. "Why kill Gwyn?"

"What are you talking about?" Brodie said.

"OK, Gene," Nick answered. "I'll put it together for you. I did some checking through the Agency's database while I was in Cleveland. I looked up all the reports on Lavender. When his body was exhumed, only one name appeared on the report stating that the coffin was empty: yours. When they killed that man in New York during the holdup of the Federal Depository, one agent had time alone with the body: you. That's where the lavender worry stone came from. You said you found it in the man's pocket, and no one doubted you. When you and Sanders went to New York, you interrogated Bernardi and shot McTavish alone. You wouldn't let Brad in the room with you. He remembered that when you entered McTavish's apartment, you had no silencer on your gun, but several minutes later in the bedroom, you did. He also didn't see you take the worry stone from McTavish's pocket, yet you claimed that's where it was. And those Intelligence reports about Bernardi stockpiling weapons all had your signature on them. You made up the whole thing."

Brodie had moved slowly to a nearby stack of crates, and sat down, putting his hands in the pockets of his black overcoat. He eyed Nick warily.

"You're letting your imagination run away with you, Nick," he said. "I don't know what you're talking about."

"Then try these on for size," Nick continued, moving in a little closer, keeping his gun leveled at Brodie. "I checked the news footage from the bombing in Cleveland. Ran the whole thing, all three-plus hours of it. News crews today go for sensationalism, and that means a lot of shots taken of the bystanders." He paused for a second. "In the crowd outside that Courthouse, immediately after the bombing, I saw your face. You were there. Felicia found the same thing when she ran the tapes of the school bus attack in Chicago."

Brodie sat motionless, staring at his partner.

"But the final piece didn't fall into place until a couple of days ago," Nick continued. "When I sent you here from New York, you indulged in your weakness for slang phrases. 'I'll catch the redeye.' Remember, Gene? That's what you said the night you were supposed to go to

Berlin, when Gwyn was killed in that explosion. I never put it together until now, but you didn't go to Berlin that night. I checked the old records and flight manifests when I got here today, and you weren't on any plane. You did, however, sign out an agency car and return it the next morning, and the mileage was exactly the same as one round trip to Glasgow. I never understood until now how you arrived on the scene of that explosion so quickly if you were supposed to be on your way out of the country."

Brodie still said nothing, but looked down at the cobblestones. Nick was feeling a rage building up within him that he hadn't felt for years. He was facing those memories that he had always pushed into the back of his mind. When he spoke, he couldn't keep the emotion and anger out of his voice.

"I should have remembered it sooner," Nick angrily continued, "but I've spent the last five years trying to put that whole night out of my mind, pretending it never happened. Then you came along and brought it all back, like a malignant cancer. Dammit, Gene, you were supposed to be my friend."

Brodie was still silent.

"It was like you knew Lavender wouldn't be in Germany," Nick continued in the same angry tone. "You even said it yourself – 'He's long gone by now.' What was I, Gene – bait? Did you use me to draw Lavender out?"

Brodie looked up at Nick.

"It wasn't supposed to happen that way," he said. "You're right, I never went to Berlin. I followed you to Scotland. You'd been putting a lot of heat on Lavender, and we heard he was getting ready to crack. I thought if we gave him an opportunity, he'd show himself, and we could grab him, so I let it get back through the underground that you were going to Glasgow that weekend and where you'd be staying. But I didn't think anyone would get hurt, and I certainly never wanted Gwyn to die. We had a dozen agents staking out the area. But Lavender must have got there before us, or had someone else set that explosion for him."

Nick paused a moment, staring coldly at Brodie.

"Did Currey know you set me up?" he demanded.

Brodie nodded his head weakly.

"He knew," he replied.

Nick took in everything his partner said, and felt somehow vindicated. Except for one thing.

"That explains what happened five years ago," Nick said. "But you still haven't told me – why now? Why this charade?"

"What charade?" Brodie responded in total innocence.

"You're indulging in your fondness for blowing smoke again, Gene," Nick replied. "I know what you and Currey have been talking about for the past few months."

Brodie narrowed his eyes a bit and furrowed his brow.

"What do you mean?" he cautiously asked.

"A little conversation about two months ago," Nick replied. "Currey had just had a meeting with the Joint Chiefs of staff, where he learned that The President's new budget didn't allocate as much funding for The Agency as before. Currey told you that there might be cutbacks at the upper management level, and a possible elimination of Bureau Chiefs like yourself. That conversation took place about three weeks before the first attack that you credited to Lavender. That's why you dropped enough clues to make Currey think Lavender was still alive. You knew his techniques as well as I did, so it was easy for you to make all those incidents look like he planned them."

Brodie's eyes widened somewhat as he wondered where Nick got his information. He took a deep breath.

"Look, Nick," he started, "it isn't like it was in the old days, when we had the world by the ass and could do no wrong, as long as we were bringing in results. We were afraid they were getting ready to shut us down. I thought if we could still prove we were needed, Congress and The President would leave us alone, let us go on like we had been. Nobody was supposed to get hurt."

"Not get hurt?" Nick asked incredulously. "What do you call maiming innocent school children, or peace demonstrators, or killing civilians in a bombing? You call that not hurting anyone?"

"I had to get their attention," Brodie said. "I had to get you back into it again, because nobody in the office today has the talent or reputation you do. I needed you back on our side for credibility. I had to resurrect Miles Lavender."

Nick stared intently into Brodie's eyes.

"You're wrong, Gene," he said. "You didn't resurrect him – you *became* Miles Lavender."

Brodie looked down at the ground.

"How deep is Currey in this time?" Nick asked.

"Not at all," Brodie answered. "I engineered this one all by myself. I recruited scum that we'd put away, ex-hit men, Aryans, disgruntled survivalists, you name it."

"Was one of them made up to look like Lavender in

that tape from Cleveland?"

Brodie nodded his head 'yes.'

"Where is he now?" Nick asked.

"On the bottom of Lake Erie, about five miles off shore," Brodie answered.

"You kill him?"

Again, Brodie nodded in the affirmative.

"But why kill Sanders?"

"What makes you think I killed Sanders?" Brodie asked cautiously.

"He left a clue, one that you didn't know about. Before he died, Brad punched in the numbers 27639 on the phone in his room. At first, I thought he was trying to call someone, and died before he could finish. Then I remembered something: when he was typing up the report of your fracas in New York, he misspelled your name. I had to correct him. He couldn't remember that you spell it "i -e" and not with a "y". That's what he was dialing on the phone – the numbers he used match the letters "b – r – o – d- y". Plus, I checked with Customs, and you didn't arrive in London until early this morning – on a direct flight from Toronto."

Brodie said nothing, but continued staring at Nick.

"Was it you who hired that nitwit private eye to follow me in Canada?" Nick asked.

"Yeah," Brodie said after a pause. "I hired Lamont to keep tabs on you."

"And you shot at me on the street last night?"

Brodie was at a loss for words.

"You might as well own up to it, Gene," Nick said. "I know how good you are with that gun. Nobody misses the target by that much unless they intend to."

"All right," Brodie finally said. "I took those shots at you last night."

"But how did you know I was going to Toronto from Cleveland?"

"I flew to Cleveland from New York and followed you when you checked out of your hotel," Brodie answered, his voice taking on a weary tone, filled with the sound of defeat. "I contacted Lamont before you got to Canada. He told me which hotel you were in. When I checked the registry, I found out Sanders was there, too."

"So you killed him and shot at me to make me think it was Lavender?"

Brodie paused a moment before answering.

"Yeah," he replied in the same tone of resignation.

Brodie sat motionless for a few minutes. Nick felt the stone cold numbness coming back over him. His work wasn't finished yet.

"So where do we go from here?" Brodie asked. "You gonna turn me in? You'll never prove any of this, and you know it. You have no proof that I did anything wrong."

Nick raised his right hand, and pointed his silenced Beretta straight at his partner and former friend. Brodie's eyes widened in terror.

"Nick, wait," he stammered.

"God, forgive me for what I am about to do," Nick thought.

"Gene, don't be an idiot," Nick said sharply. "Put away the gun!"

Brodie stood up slowly from the crate, taking his empty hands out of his pockets, palms forward, and raised them as high as his shoulders, trying to figure out what Nick was talking about.

Gun? What gun? My gun's still in my holster, for Christ's sake! What the hell is he doing?

"Dammit, Gene, drop the gun!" Nick ordered.

The first shot from Nick's Beretta caught Brodie in the upper left chest, sending him backwards over the crate he had been sitting on, and the second one caught him square in the middle of his chest as he was falling. He lay on his back on the cobblestones.

Nick turned off the tape recorder in his wristband and approached Brodie's body. He stood over the lifeless remains and pointed his gun at Brodie's head. Nick's face had turned to stone once again.

"And one more for Gwyn," he said quietly as he planted one last 9mm slug between Brodie's eyes.

Nick holstered his gun, took a handkerchief from his pocket, and wrapped it around his right hand. Kneeling down, he reached under Brodie's coat, took out his weapon, and placed it in the dead man's outstretched palm. Wrapping Brodie's hand around the weapon, Nick placed the right forefinger on the trigger. He raised the weapon, taking aim at a spot across the alley near where he had been standing and squeezed Brodie's finger on the trigger twice, imbedding two slugs from his gun into the wall of the building. He then put Brodie's hand back down on the ground.

Nick walked calmly out of the alley, his shoes making a clopping sound on the cobblestones, stopping long enough to fire up a Winston. He looked once again at the gold lighter before putting it back in his pocket, and grinned. Maybe it really was a good luck charm, after all. When he was in the car, he took off the recorder wristwatch and tucked into his breast pocket.

Best insurance in the world. Now maybe they'll leave me the hell alone, he thought.

Nick checked the time: 10:00 p.m. That meant it was 5:00 on Key Largo, and the dinner crowd would just be starting to fill up Calhoun's. If he hurried, he could make the redeye back to Miami and be home by morning.

* * *

7:00 a.m. Funny, but Nick had never noticed that the sunrises on The Keys were just as pretty as the sunsets. He'd have to get up earlier more often.

Nick unlocked the door to his condo and stepped inside, wondering if anyone was there. He heard a sound coming from the master bedroom, and looked up to see Felicia walking down the stairs, rubbing sleep from her eyes. He noticed that she still didn't believe in wearing nightgowns. Felicia saw Nick standing by the door, stopped and looked at him for a moment. A smile slowly spread across her face. She hurried down the rest of the stairs and flung her arms around him.

After a long embrace, she leaned back and looked into his eyes.

"Hiya, tough guy," she said with a warm smile. "Now forever?"

"Now forever," he replied.

He kissed Felicia as though he hadn't seen her in years, and gently rubbed his hands over her naked back. He realized this was what he had missed – someone to care for, to share his life with. Nick stopped kissing Felicia and looked into her soft brown eyes.

"You know what we're going to do now?" he asked softly.

"What?" she responded, meeting his dreamy-eyed gaze.

"We're going upstairs, I'm going to lie down and close my eyes, and when I wake up, I want to find you next to me – forever," he answered.

Life started to settle into a nice routine for the two of them over the next few months. Nick still played innkeeper at Calhoun's, and brought Felicia into the business to share that part of his life. Between bouts of playing host and hostess to the clientele at the yacht club, they started spending more time on Nick's boat, enjoying the natural beauty of the gulf coast. It was something that Nick had always been aware of, but now appreciated anew. He also starting noticing and appreciating other little things that had previously escaped his attention.

That seemed to define the direction Nick's life was taking – he now had a course mapped out, and wasn't about to change his destination or his quest for tranquility in his private corner of paradise. Felicia was now a vital part of his existence and she was as happy to be with him as he was to be with her. Nick hadn't felt this kind of happiness or satisfaction since Gwyn had died, and he vowed to do whatever he had to do to keep the feeling alive. He was also sure he wouldn't have any more interference from his former employer.

At least, that's what Nick Seven thought.

- *Eight* -

The autumn night had a chill in the air, helped by the slight mist of fog rolling in. It was dark in the alley, with only the stray light from a nearby streetlamp to illuminate the dark. Nick walked slowly, steadily into the cobblestoned alley, his 9mm Beretta in his right hand, his eyes peering into the shadows, adjusting to the dim light and waiting for something to move. He heard the sound of movement to his right, near the delivery entrance to a market. Nick stopped walking, and trained his eyes and weapon in the direction of the sounds. A lone figure slowly, cautiously backed into the alley, checking to see if he was alone. Nick stood silently, waiting for the man to come into range. When he did, Nick called out to him.

"Stop where you are!" he commanded. "CIA. You're under arrest. Turn around, and raise your hands!"

The man quickly turned around, and Nick saw that he was brandishing a Glock semi-automatic pistol, poised to shoot.

Nick fired three shots in rapid succession, the impact of the bullets forcing the man backwards a few steps, where he came to rest on the ground against some garbage cans. Nick slowly approached the body, and took a good look at the face of his prey.

It was his own face on the dead man!

Nick suddenly bolted upright in bed, gasping for air, his hands trembling. He was sweating profusely.

Damn thermostat's set for 68 degrees, and I'm sweating, for Christ's sake! he thought.

He sat on the edge of the bed, leaned forward, and rested his head in the palms of his hands, trying to regain his composure and get his breathing and pulse rate back under control. Next to him, Felicia awoke and saw Nick sitting on the edge of the bed. She scooted over to him.

"What's wrong, Hon?" she asked in her sleepy Carribean accent.

Nick was taking some deep breaths.

"Couldn't sleep," he finally managed to say. "Bad dream."

"You mean same dream?" she gently asked.

Nick nodded in the affirmative, and Felicia came closer, wrapping her arms around him in comfort. After a few minutes, she spoke.

"Nick," she said, "it's OK. You just havin' bad dreams is all."

"But why, after all this time?" he asked. "Six months. I should be over it by now. I've killed before and never lost any sleep. Why is this one bothering me?"

"Because you killed Brodie, and he used to be your friend," Felicia answered while gently rubbing his shoulders. "You just feelin' guilty, all ate up inside because he turned on you and you didn't want that. Nick..."

She forced him to look at her, and bore into him with her soft, deep brown eyes.

"You did the right thing," she finally said. "If it hadn't been him, it would've been you lyin' in that alley in London. Brodie wasn't no friend to set you up like he did, to use you like he did. You just doin' what you had to do. Besides," she paused, smiling coyly, "where would we be if you hadn't ?"

Nick finally managed a small smile, and put his arm around her.

"You're right," he said. "And thank you. Hey, I've got an idea. The sun's coming up. How about we take the boat out and have breakfast on the bay?"

"How 'bout you come back under these covers and wake me proper first?" she teased, pulling him back into bed with her.

Felicia began kissing him, and moving her hands all along his body. He responded to her touch, and was completely lost in her beauty and insatiable appetite. Even first thing in the morning, Nick found Felicia irresistible. He passionately kissed her, moving his mouth and hands along her upper body as she continued to arouse him with her hands. Nick gently rolled Felicia over on her back, and as she pulled her knees upward towards her body, he guided himself inside her and began making love to her, causing Felicia to moan with pleasure.

* * *

Nick went to the gym of his condo complex later that morning, to try and work out some of his frustrations. After all these months had passed and things were going so well for the two of them, Nick couldn't figure out why he was still carrying the memory of what he had done. Maybe it was true that memories died last. As he worked out in the gym, he remembered what Felicia had said, and knew she was right. It had been a case of kill or be killed, just like it had been when Nick finally caught up with Miles Lavender. Maybe he should be seeing a psychiatrist. After a hard hour of working out with weights and walking from hell to eternity on the treadmill, Nick was feeling no better than when he came in. Only sore.

A hot shower and a change of clothes later, Nick was at the marina. He noticed the last time he took his Bayliner out for a cruise that the fuel injectors were clogged, so he thought he'd try to lose himself in working on the boat's engine. He started thinking again about the last six months – how he'd been suckered by the Agency into coming back to active duty only to chase a ghost halfway around the world, how he finally put the puzzle together, how he killed his former partner in London and avenged the death of his wife, and how he came back to Key Largo, his Yacht Club, and Felicia, the girl he realized he always wanted but never pursued. Life was just starting to get good again.

Nick was lost in thought about things best left forgotten when a voice brought him back to earth.

"Excuse me," a young voice said. "Are you Mr. Seven?"

Nick took his head out of the engine compartment and looked up on the dock. There he saw a young girl, probably not more than 20, attractive, with long auburn hair streaked by the Florida sun, and green eyes. She looked like any of the hundreds of kids you'd find cluttering up the beach on any given Spring break.

"Yeah," he said. "I'm Nick Seven. And you are…"

"Jennifer," she said after a pause. "Jennifer Brinkman. Can we talk?"

"Sure," Nick said. "You start."

"Not here," she said. "Isn't there someplace more private, like maybe in your boat?"

No way I'm taking this piece of jailbait into my boat! Nick thought.

"Better idea," he said, pointing towards Calhoun's. "Let's go inside. I was getting too hot out here anyway."

He climbed onto the deck and they started walking towards the club.

"Do you think they'll let me in?" Jennifer asked.

"No problem," Nick answered. "The owner's a personal friend of mine."

They sat in the restaurant side of Calhoun's, where Nick ordered iced tea for himself and Diet Coke for the girl. After lighting a cigarette, Nick began the conversation.

"So," he said. "What did you want to talk to me about? A summer job? I can always use another good waitress."

The girl was staring intently at the design on the carpet. She shook her head 'no.' Finally, she looked up at him.

"I need your help," she said.

"With what?"

"I'm Jennifer Brinkman."

"Yeah," Nick replied. "We've established that. You Jennifer, me Nick. So what's the problem?"

Jennifer paused a moment before continuing. She began playing with the ruby ring on her right hand, twisting it around her finger.

"I'm being blackmailed," she finally said.

"You?" Nick asked in genuine surprise. "What could a kid like you have done that would be worth blackmailing?"

"You see," she said at length, obviously embarassed, "I went to this party with some friends a couple of weeks ago. Things got a little out of hand, there was a lot of drinking, and somehow, I was videotaped having sex with some of the guys there."

Nick pondered this for a moment.

"Were you raped?" he finally asked as gently as he could.

"Mr. Seven," Jennifer said, "I don't remember. Someone must have put something into my drink. All I know is, the tape was sent to me, along with a note demanding $500,000.00."

Nick let out a low whistle.

"Where do they expect you to come up with that kind of scratch?" he asked.

"Mr. Seven," she said, "my father is Paul Brinkman."

Nick raised his eyebrows.

"THE Paul Brinkman? The newspaper publisher?"

She nodded her head yes.

"So what's the problem?" Nick asked. "I know your old man's good for the money. Why not explain what happened and have him bail you out?"

"You don't understand," she said. "Daddy's got a very bad temper. He'd go ballistic if he ever found out about this."

"Is that why you haven't told the police?"

"Yes," she answered, then looked at Nick in surprise. "How did you know I hadn't talked to the police?"

"If you had, you wouldn't be here."

"Daddy knows so many important people, it would be impossible to keep it from him if I went to the police. He'd positively die if he ever saw that tape. Mr. Seven, I don't know what they gave me, but on that tape, I look like I'm having the time of my life."

Nick paused and took a puff on his cigarette.

"Were you?" He asked.

Jennifer looked as though she were about to cry.

"Sorry," Nick said. "I had to ask. Where was this party you went to, and who took you?"

"It was in Miami. I went with a guy I know from school, Carl Lonergan. The apartment was somewhere on Biscayne Boulevard. I don't know the address, but it was two weeks ago Thursday."

"OK," Nick said, "that's a start. But how did you happen to pick me as your savior?"

"I read about you," Jennifer said.

Nick's eyes narrowed.

"Read about me where?" he asked cautiously.

"In an article Daddy's paper is getting ready to publish," she said. "I'm studying journalism in college, and one of the reporters thought he'd make points with the boss' daughter by showing me the research on a series of articles Daddy wants to run exposing the CIA. Your name was in the article, along with some information about you."

"What kind of information?" Nick warily asked.

"About how you're a former CIA agent, how you've

killed people, and how you came here to hide from your past. There was some other stuff in there, too, about some guy that was your partner that they found dead in England, and how his murder was never solved."

Nick slumped back in his chair.

Damn! he thought, *I knew things were going too well.*

"Would you excuse me for a minute?" he asked, getting up from the table.

Nick walked across the room to the bar. Felicia approached him from the inside of the bar, and motioned her head towards Jennifer.

"Who's the cheerleader?" she asked.

"A girl who says her name is Jennifer Brinkman," Nick answered. "Says she's being blackmailed. Says her old man is Paul Brinkman. You know – THE Paul Brinkman, the newspaper guy. Says she can't ask the old man for the payoff and she wants me to help her."

"So what she think you are – The Salvation Army? Why she come knockin' at your door?"

"She says she found my name in some article her old man plans to run about the CIA. She claims I'm in the article, along with info about a certain Agency Bureau Chief that was found murdered in London six months ago."

This time it was Felicia's turn to whistle.

"You think she's straight?" Felicia asked.

"I don't know," Nick answered. "Either she's on the level, or a reporter Brinkman sent in here to dig up more dirt for that story. Either way, I have to find out."

"Wait a minute, Hon," Felicia protested. "You don't need to get mixed up in this mess."

"I know," Nick answered, "but I can't have my life laid out for everyone to see, either. We've worked too hard for that."

Nick went back to the table and sat down.

"Do you have the tape?" he asked Jennifer.

"Yes," she answered.

"I'll have to see it."

Jennifer got a look of mortification on her face, and turned pale.

"Don't worry," Nick said, "I want to see if I can find out who shot it, or identify anyone in it. Trust me."

Jennifer was still fascinated by the design on the carpet and obsessed with twirling the ruby ring around her finger. Finally, she opened her handbag and took out a videotape, sliding it across the table to Nick. He was about to take it, when she stopped him.

"Are you sure you have to watch it?" she asked.

"I'm sure," he answered.

The girl released her grip on the tape, and Nick picked it up to examine it. There were no markings on it, except for the brand name, which wouldn't help him, since you could buy it at any convenience store.

"Do you still have the note that came with it?"

She reached into her handbag again, withdrew a piece of paper, and slid it across the table. Nick looked at it. It was not written, but typed on a word processor, also the type found in any home or office. He recited the note aloud.

$500,000.00 or this tape goes on the market. Get the money, we'll be in touch.

He put the note down.

"Have they tried to contact you yet?" he asked.

"No," she said. "What do you think they meant when they said 'on the market'?"

"It means they'll sell it to some distributor, and you'll be doing your thing in thousands of bedrooms across America."

The girl looked like she was going to pass out.

"Oh, no!" she moaned. "We can't let that happen!"

"When they make contact, you call me. Agree to whatever they want. I'll see what I can find out, and be in touch. Where can I reach you?"

"It would be better if I called you," she said.

"I wouldn't like that," Nick responded. "You want me to help you, you play by my rules. Now, where can I reach you?"

After thinking for a moment, Jennifer wrote her number on a cocktail napkin, and passed it to Nick.

"This your old man's place?" he asked.

"No," she said, "I have my own condo."

"Of course you do," Nick said, chuckling.

Nick and Jennifer rose from the table, Jennifer shaking Nick's hand as she parted.

At least she's had training in the social graces, he thought.

Nick went back to the bar, and Felicia approached him.

"So what you do now?" she asked.

Nick thought for a minute.

"Get Raul to cover the bar," he answered, "and come with me."

"Where we goin'?" she asked.

Nick grinned wickedly.

"To the movies," he answered.

- *Nine* -

Nick and Felicia viewed the tape back in the condo. It looked like typical home video stuff, with no redeeming production values, save for some cheesy background music. The girl was right – she looked like she was thoroughly enjoying herself. Nick paused the tape in several places, and photographed any faces that appeared, including the girl's. A half hour after the tape was over, Nick sat up in bed, lit a cigarette, and asked Felicia what she thought.

"You were great as always," she lazily answered, slowly rubbing her hand on his leg.

"I meant the tape!" he asked in mock annoyance.

"Oh," she replied. "Nothin' I'd pay to see."

"Thanks a lot," he said. "You're a big help."

She was about to spar further with him when the phone rang. Nick answered it.

"Yeah," he said, "this is Mr. Seven. Who wants to know? Really. When? Yeah, I can drop by."

"Who was it?" Felicia asked as he hung up the phone.

"Paul Brinkman's personal secretary," Nick answered. "His Royal Highness requests a private audience with me at his office in an hour."

"You goin'?" she asked.

"Why not?" he answered. "Maybe the old man knows more than his little girl is letting on."

An hour later, Nick was ushered into the palatial office of Paul Brinkman, Publisher. Nick looked around the office, noting the antique furnishings and expensive oil paintings on the wall. He also noticed the security camera hidden behind Brinkman's massive oak desk. He wondered where the microphones were planted.

Nick was offered a seat, and a drink. Brinkman was a throwback to a bygone era, a cross between William Randolph Hearst and General Patton – take no prisoners, and no bullshit. The media magnate began with some small talk.

"Finest 12-year-old single-malt Scotch you can get," he began, toasting Nick by raising his lead crystal glass.

Nick followed suit, and took a sip. Not as good as Grouse, but it would do.

"So," Brinkman continued, "how's business at Calhoun's?"

"Not bad," Nick replied. "Busy enough to keep me off the streets at night. And you?"

"Getting better everyday. In fact, we're gearing up to launch another publication."

"How many periodicals do you publish now – three?"

"I see you've done your homework. That's right. All of them do well, especially the World Inquirer, our tabloid. Ever read that one?"

"Only when I line the garbage can."

Brinkman's eyes narrowed a bit, and he let out a small laugh.

"Never underestimate the buying power of the

American people," he answered. "I wouldn't say I'm proudest of that one, but I just give this country what it wants – sex and scandal. Lots of it."

"And the beat goes on," Nick replied, raising his glass to Brinkman before taking another sip.

Apparently the small talk was over, as Brinkman came right to the point of his summons.

"I understand you've been seeing my daughter, Mr. Seven," he said.

"Not exactly," Nick answered. "She came to see me."

"About what?" Brinkman demanded.

"Why?" Nick responded, non-plussed.

"Because she's my daughter, and I'm asking."

"Suppose I said it's none of your business?"

"Suppose I said I could make your business my business?"

"Nah," Nick said, "you wouldn't like the hours."

Brinkman leaned towards the desk and narrowed his eyes, taking on a look of granite.

"Now, look, Seven," he said with a hard edge to his voice. "I'm a man who's used to getting what he wants, and I don't care who I have to step on to get it. Understand?"

Nick sat and looked at Brinkman, not responding. He calmly took a sip of Scotch.

"OK," Brinkman finally said. "You like to play hardball? Let's play."

He picked up a folder from his desk, and started reading aloud.

"Nicholas Timothy Seven," he began. "42 years old. Born in Detroit. Parents both deceased. Served in the

Intelligence Division of the U.S. Army, leaving with the rank of Major. Law degree from George Washington University. Headed European operations for the CIA, where he specialized in hunting down terrorists. Married once, but wife died under mysterious circumstances. Should I go on?"

Nick said nothing, so Brinkman continued.

"Relocated to Key Largo, currently the owner of Calhoun's. Took a sudden trip six months ago, during which time a CIA Bureau Chief named Eugene Brodie was found murdered in London, also under mysterious circumstances. Murder never solved. Returned to Key Largo, where he's been keeping house with a woman from Barbados named Felicia Hagens, who is also a former CIA operative. Well, what do you have to say now?"

Nick calmly took another sip of Scotch.

"You left out my shoe size," he responded.

"Let's not do this the hard way, Mr. Seven," Brinkman said. "This is only a rough draft of what I can dig up on you. I'm preparing a complete exposé on the CIA, from its inception as the OSS during World War II right up to the present, with everything in between. The information from an insider who was there would be quite valuable to me."

"Sorry, but I don't snoop and tell," Nick said. "And your dossier isn't quite complete. You also left out that I don't threaten worth a shit."

"All right," Brinkman said. "Have it your way – for now. I just hope you're as lucky as you are cocky."

Nick got up from his chair.

"Thanks for the drink," he said. "Stop by my place sometime and I'll return the favor."

Nick left the office. When the door was closed, Brinkman picked up his phone.

"Send Roberts in here," he told his secretary. "And get me Newsome at Immigration."

Nick returned to his condo, and took the disc from the digital camera he used to photograph the images on the video tape. He ran it through his computer, and in a few minutes he had printed closeups of the people involved in the orgy. He looked closely at Jennifer Brinkman's face, and began to put some credence in her story – although seemingly enjoying the activity, her eyes had a glazed, drugged look to them. He also noticed something else at the end of the tape that caught his attention. There was a copyright mark with the current year, assigned to "Climaxxx Films."

He began to think that the film had already been sold, the perpetrators had collected their money, and were now bleeding the girl for more. Playing both ends against the middle. Nick had to find out if the tape was actually on the market. He gathered up the photos and decided to drive back to Miami.

It was a warm, clear day, so Nick put the top down on his Mustang during the forty-five-minute drive up Highway 1. His first stop was at the office of an acquaintance of his from the old days, a local film and video distributor named Harry Trent. "Trent Productions" was no MGM, but Harry managed to make a decent living selling videos of all kinds to local stores, as well as helping film companies from Hollywood find locations and local talent when they came to Southern Florida to make a movie or TV show. His office was located in an old building on Indianola Avenue, the kind that the city hadn't gotten around to condemning yet.

The two men shook hands, Harry commenting that it had been a long time. He ushered Nick into his office, and closed the door.

"So," Harry Trent began, "to what do I owe the pleasure?"

"I'm looking for some information about a sleaze factory named Climaxxx Films," Nick answered. "Ever hear of them?"

"Sure," Harry answered. "We handle some of their stuff. Mostly home-grown product, sent in by aspiring Spielbergs from across the country. Everybody with a video camera thinks they can make it in the movies these days."

"Where do they operate out of?"

"San Francisco. People send in their home movies, Climaxxx pays $500 cash up front for the rights, then sells copies to anyone and everyone, either through stores or the internet. Why do you want to know about them?"

Nick took the pictures from his pocket, and passed them along to Trent.

"Any of these people look familiar?" he asked.

Trent looked at the pictures for a minute, shuffling them a few times, finally coming back to the one of Jennifer Brinkman. He nodded his head yes.

"This one," he said. "I've seen her before."

"In a video?" Nick asked.

"Yeah," Trent answered. "She's been in several we got

from Climaxxx."

"You mean recently?"

"No, I mean some we've had for a few years. Big sellers, too."

"Do you still have any of them left?"

Harry got up and left the office. In a few minutes he returned with six video tapes, all in garishly colored boxes showing scenes of the action contained on the tapes inside. Nick looked at the boxes, and recognized the girl's face on each one.

"Which tape is the oldest one?"

Trent looked at the dates on the tapes, and handed one to Nick.

"This one," he said. "Copyrighted two years ago. You wanna borrow these?"

"Just this one," Nick said. "I'll get it back to you in a couple of days. Do you recognize any of the other faces I showed you?"

Trent shook his head 'no.'

"Sorry, Nick," he said, "but it's not the guys' faces anyone is interested in."

Nick chuckled.

"No, I guess not," he said, standing up. "By the way, this girl got a stage name?"

"Yeah," Trent answered, looking at the box. "Monica Foxx – with two x's."

"Tell me, Harry," Nick asked. "How does a nice guy like you end up selling this kind of stuff?"

Trent shrugged his shoulders.

"It's a tough market today, Nick," he answered. "You go where the money is."

"How about your suppliers?" Nick asked. "Are they tough, too?"

"They can be persuasive," Trent answered. "But I'm still here."

"Thanks, Harry," he said, shaking hands. "You've been a big help, and I owe you one."

"Forget it," Harry said. "This pays back the one I owe you from a few years ago when you helped me with that creep from the IRS."

Nick was leaving the office building, and as he approached his car, he noticed someone looking inside, peering through the tinted glass. There was a row of Cypress trees lining the street. Nick walked softly along the sidewalk, found a tree ten feet from his car, and stood beside it. The man sizing up Nick's car didn't know he had company. Nick took the keyless remote from his pocket, held it towards the car, and pressed the red horn button.

The would-be thief jumped up in surprise as the car's horn started blasting. Nick rushed up behind him, grabbed the man, and forced him face down over the hood, pinning him down by holding his left arm behind his back.

"Hey, man!" the guy exclaimed, struggling to get free. "You're hurting me!"

"What a shame," Nick answered. "Who sent you here?"

"Nobody," the guy answered through clenched teeth. "I was just gonna boost the stereo, that's all."

Nick twisted the guy's arm higher towards his shoulder, and he cried out in more pain.

"You're starting to piss me off with these wrong answers," Nick said. "Now, who sent you?"

After a brief pause, the guy managed to say "Brinkman!"

Nick released his grip on the man's arm, pulled him to his feet, turned him around, and threw him back down on the hood, face up this time, wrapping his left hand around the man's throat.

"Now listen good," Nick said intently. "I told your boss, and now I'm telling you: I don't take threats well, and I get even more annoyed when people follow me. Understand?"

The man nodded yes. Nick released his death grip on the man's windpipe, pulled him up from the car, and stepped back.

"Beat it!" Nick ordered. The man took off down the street.

Nick drove a few blocks until a found a diner, where he went inside to get a cup of coffee. As he drank his coffee and had a cigarette, he recounted what he had learned so far. The video tape boxes showed a girl that looked like Jennifer Brinkman, but could have been someone else. Was the girl scamming him about the blackmail? Was she really 'Monica Foxx,' porn star extraordinare? Nick had one more lead to follow up on.

He found a listing for Carl Lonergan in the phone book on Biscayne Boulevard. Nick drove to the address, a high-rise luxury apartment building. It was obvious that a college student couldn't afford digs like these without help from mom and dad – or another source of income.

There was no doorman on duty, so Nick checked the mailboxes, finding one for a "C. Lonergan" in 902. He took the elevator to the 9th floor, found #902, and leaned close to the door, listening for the sound of anyone inside. Hearing nothing, he knocked, but got no answer. He knocked again, harder this time. Still no answer.

Looking around to be sure there were no witnesses, Nick took a ' burglar's tool' from his pocket, jimmied the lock, and went inside. The place was a state-of-the art modern equivalent to a bachelor pad. Nick found the bedroom, and looked around, immediately spotting a video camera hidden behind a two-way mirror in the dresser. Further snooping found a cache of video tapes, unlabeled. Nick could only guess what was on them. He removed a small camera from his pocket, took pictures from every angle of the bedroom, then left the apartment. Nick went back to his car, and noticed the time. 4:00. He decided to drive back to Key Largo.

The parking lot was full at Calhoun's, meaning a good dinner crowd tonight. Nick parked in his reserved spot and went inside. Once in the restaurant, he heard the sound of raised voices coming from the bar. One of them sounded very familiar.

He quickly entered the bar, and saw Felicia in a heated argument with a man wearing a three-piece suit. Nick immediately sized him up as a Federal Agent, since he used to get his clothes from the same tailor. From what he could hear, Felicia had obviously picked up some choice words from all those drunken sailors she bounced out of that bar in Barbados.

"What the hell's going on here?" Nick asked loudly as he approached the squabbling pair.

"This 'suit' says I got no right to work here!" Felicia angrily responded.

"Who are you?" Nick demanded.

"Phillip Newsome, Immigration and Naturalization Services," the man answered, showing his identification. "And who might you be?"

"Nick Seven," he responded, "owner and proprietor, that's who the hell I might be. What's the problem?"

"We've had a complaint that you have illegal immigrants working here," Newsome replied. "Specifically, your barmaid."

Nick took a deep breath, resisting the urge to punch Newsome's lights out.

"If you are referring to Ms. Hagens," he replied tersely, "she has a work visa issued by your department six months ago. It is valid for another six months. I presume she showed you her green card."

Newsome nodded in the affirmative.

"Then I suggest," Nick said, keeping his temper under control, "that unless you're going to order dinner, you get the hell out of here."

"You understand, of course," Newsome explained, "that we have to check out all complaints."

"Yeah," Nick said, "I understand."

Newsome left and Nick approached Felicia, who was still seething with anger.

"Come on," he said, "let's eat."

They sat at his usual table overlooking the marina. Nick ordered shark steaks and drinks for both of them (making hers a double rum), and lit a cigarette.

"Will you relax?" he finally said.

"I don't like those damn suits comin' in here pushin' me around," Felicia replied, still angry. "I got enough of that in the Agency."

"You have to expect visits from the INS if you're here on a visa," Nick answered.

"But the only way I become a citizen is if –"

She looked at Nick, who had assumed his usual pose – right leg crossed over his left, chin cupped in his left hand, cigarette in his right, with a grin on his face.

"Do you mean–" she started to ask.

"Maybe," he replied coyly. "In the meantime, you want to know what I found out today?"

"Sure," she replied. "Anything to take my mind off this mess."

"Our little miss cheerleader may not be the innocent she claims to be," Nick said. "I paid a call on Harry Trent in Miami, and he showed me some video tapes from a porn company in San Francisco. The pictures on the box look like the Brinkman girl, only she goes by the name Monica Foxx – with two x's. The oldest tape came out about two years ago."

"You still think she's on the level?" Felicia asked.

"I'm not sure," Nick answered. "But there's something else. Brinkman Sr. read me some of the contents of that file he has for his planned expose on The Agency. I don't know where he got his information, but he knows all about me – and you."

"Me?"

Nick nodded his head slowly.

"That's probably why you got the roust from that dweeb from INS," he said. "I'd bet a month's pay that Brinkman sicced him on you."

"So how we find out who's tellin' the truth here?"

"Beats the hell out of me. Brinkman had me followed this afternoon by some punk, probably one of his reporters, so he knows I visited Trent. I also got into the apartment where the girl said the alleged party took place, and found a video camera hidden in the bedroom."

"So what you thinkin'?"

Nick took a puff on his cigarette and exhaled slowly.

"I looked at the girl's face on that tape, and she had a glazed look in her eyes, like she was high on something," he replied. "Maybe she was a willing participant, maybe not. Maybe she really is a porn star and this is Brinkman's way of getting to me. I've got to find out who's been feeding him information from Langley."

"But how?"

"I don't know yet. There must be somebody there who still owes me a favor, and won't tell The Old Man about it. I just have to figure out who to ask."

"You think Currey has a mole in the organization?"

Nick looked intently at Felicia for a moment, remembering what had happened in London six months earlier.

"It wouldn't be the first time," he replied.

- *Ten* -

Nick went to his office, took the cocktail napkin with Jennifer Brinkman's phone number from his pocket and dialed the number. After a few rings, a woman answered.

"Jennifer Brinkman, please," Nick said.

"Who?" the woman asked.

"Jennifer Brinkman," Nick repeated. "This is 576-9802, isn't it?"

"Yes, but there's no one named Jennifer here," the woman responded.

"I see," Nick said. "Excuse me, but is this a private residence?"

"No," the woman said, "this is a payphone outside Calhoun's Yacht Club on the Marina."

Nick hung up the phone.

Damn! he thought. *You really played me. All right, if I can't call you, I'll just have to find you.*

Nick went back to the bar, got himself a drink and resumed his seat by the window. Too late to do any searching tonight. He sat back, lit a cigarette, listened to the smooth jazz he always had playing on the sound system, and surveyed the crowd of patrons, waving hello to some of the regulars. As he looked around, something seemed out of place. He caught the attention of Raul from behind the bar, and motioned him to come over.

"Another drink, Chief?" the young Cuban asked.

"Yeah," Nick answered, "but have Felicia bring it to me."

Felicia came to the table a few minutes later, and handed Nick another bourbon and ginger ale. He asked her to sit down.

"I've been watching the customers, and I think we have our own mole in our midst," he said.

"Who?" Felicia asked.

"Blonde sitting at the bar. You can't miss her — bleached hair, too much makeup, flashy jewelry, and wearing a mini-skirt that rides halfway up her ass."

"I saw her. What she doin' that makes you so suspicious?"

"She keeps reaching into her handbag on the bar, moving it around, like she's trying to record conversations."

"You want I throw her ass out?"

"No," said Nick, "not yet. Not until we have a reason to."

"But she not doin' anythin' but sittin' and drinkin'. You think she's one of Brinkman's stooges?"

"Probably. Here's what I want you to do. Have Raul mix up one of those Cuban Hurricanes of his, you know, the drink that's pure alcohol and hits you like a freight train. Have him put one of these into it."

Nick reached into his pocket, withdrew a small bottle of pills, took one out, and slid it across the table to Felicia.

"What is it?" she asked.

"Phenobarbital," Nick answered. "My doctor gave

them to me so I could get some sleep at night because of all the nightmares. Have Raul tell her the drink is from Mr. Brady at the end of the bar."

"Mr. Brady?" Felicia asked in surprise. She leaned over the table and lowered her voice. "Nick, he's gay!"

"I know that," Nick said, "and you and old man Brady know it, but she doesn't. Tell Brady after she gets the drink to sit next to her and make conversation."

"But he's gay! What he want with a hot-lookin' mama like that?"

"Just tell him that if he does it, I won't press him to pay his bar tab this month."

"I hope you know what you're doin'," Felicia said, getting up.

That makes two of us, Nick thought.

Nick sat back, sipped his drink, and watched the fun begin. Right on schedule, Raul delivered the drink in a tall glass, and explained that the older gentleman at the end of the bar had sent it over with his compliments. The woman looked at Mr. Brady, who dressed like a refugee from the 70's, complete with powder-blue leisure suit and matching white shoes and belt. She smiled, raised her glass and took a sip. On cue, Mr. Brady approached with his own drink, and took the stool next to her. They began talking, the woman moving the handbag again, closer to Mr. Brady.

Come on, Nick thought. *Drink up.*

The more of the Hurricane the woman consumed, the more tipsy she became. Soon her voice started to get loud, followed by raucous laughter at something Mr. Brady said to her. Within a few minutes, she was giggling hysterically, and falling all over the old man. Nick got up from his chair, and approached the pair.

"Give me another one of these!" the woman called out to Raul.

"Excuse me, miss," Nick began, "but I think you've had enough for one night." She started to argue with him, but he wouldn't let her. "Raul, call a cab for the young lady, and see that she gets in it."

"Right away, Chief," Raul said, picking up the phone.

A few minutes later the cab arrived. Raul and Felicia escorted the woman outside. She was still arguing loudly.

"Thanks, Mr. Brady," Nick said to the old man.

"My pleasure," he answered. "Anything for a friend and a month's worth of free drinks!"

Nick laughed and went back to his table. Felicia came over and sat down.

"Nice job," she said. "You should do this for a livin'."

"I used to, remember?"

"Here," she said, handing him a micro-cassette tape.

"Where did you get this?" Nick asked.

"From the tape recorder in her purse."

"You searched her purse?"

"Me? Of course not!" Felicia answered with mock indignation. "But I had to get her address to give to the cabbie, didn't I?"

"Maybe YOU should do this for a living," Nick said.

Felicia shook her hand in a defiant 'no.'

"Been there, done that, Hon," she said.

"By the way, I tried calling that number the Brinkman girl gave me, and it was a phony. I guess I'll have to do this the hard way. I wonder if Bones McCoy is still working the streets for the Agency?"

"McCoy?" Felicia asked, surprised. "What you want with him?"

"Information," Nick answered. "Maybe he can find out who supplied my life story to Brinkman."

"But you haven't seen McCoy in years. How you expect to find him? He may not even be alive."

"Simple," Nick said. "I'll call him."

Nick went back to his office, took out a rolodex from a locked drawer in his desk, looked up the number he needed, and picked up the phone. The number he dialed was for a paging service, the kind that accepted voice messages. After the tone, he left his message.

"Bones, this is your cousin Otis. Call me at 305-576-1936. It's a family emergency."

He hung up and waited. Fifteen minutes later, the phone rang. It was McCoy.

"Glad to see you're still among the living," Nick said.

"Shit, man," McCoy answered, "takes more than bullets to kill Superman. Never expected to hear from you, though. What have you been up to?"

"That's not important," Nick answered. "What's more important is what someone else has been up to."

"Who?"

"Can't talk about it over the phone. Where are you working these days?"

"I'm in Atlanta, working on loan out to the DEA."

"Can we get together and talk?"

"Sure. How soon, and where?"

"As soon as possible. Can you get away and catch a plane to Miami?"

"Tomorrow afternoon soon enough?"

"It'll have to be."

Nick gave McCoy the address of a restaurant in the Kendall section of Miami, and made a date for 1:00 the following afternoon. He rejoined Felicia at his table.

"Did you get him?" she asked.

"Yeah. I'm meeting him tomorrow afternoon. Ya know, talking to Bones, about his being undercover, gave me an idea. How would you like to get back into action?"

"How?"

"By getting into Brinkman's office and finding out what you can."

"But how do I do that?"

"How good are you at cleaning?"

* * *

Nick had some time to kill the next morning before his meeting with McCoy, so he decided to check something on the two video tapes he had. After pouring a cup of coffee, he watched part of the tape the girl had given him. He froze the action where he could see where the scene was shot, and held up the photographs he had taken in Carl Lonergan's apartment. They weren't even close, which meant the film the girl said she was being blackmailed with was actually shot somewhere else. Nick changed tapes and looked at the one he borrowed from Trent. Monica Foxx, as she was called, was a dead ringer for the alleged Jennifer Brinkman. Nick watched some of the action on the screen for a few minutes when Felicia walked into the room, standing behind him.

"Oooh," she said, looking at the screen. "That look like

fun. We have to try that position sometime, Hon."

Nick looked up and gave her a wicked grin.

"I was thinking about a trapeze instead," he teased.

Felicia gave a thoughtful look.

"That sound like fun, too," she said.

She poured herself a cup of coffee and sat down next to Nick on the sofa.

"That sure look like the same girl we saw in that other flick," she said.

"Yeah," Nick replied, freezing the picture on a closeup of Monica Foxx's face. "Little Miss Cheerleader."

He stopped the tape and rewound it. After taking a sip of coffee he lit a cigarette.

"There's something else," Nick said. "That first tape, the so-called blackmail piece, wasn't shot at the apartment where the girl said it was. The scene of the action doesn't match what I saw there."

"So how you find this bimbo if she give you a wrong phone number?" Felicia asked.

"Maybe I'll run into her on the street," Nick joked.

"What time you meetin' McCoy?"

Nick looked at his watch.

"In about an hour and half," he said. "I'd better get going."

He leaned over and kissed Felicia.

"Be careful tonight," he said.

"YOU be careful, too," she replied.

Nick arrived at The Florentine restaurant a few minutes before 1:00 He ordered coffee, and killed some time by reading a copy of The Weekly Impact, a free tabloid that some conservatives would call radical because of its underground nature and left-of-center stand on current events. Nick always got a laugh out of some of the quirkier news stories the paper reported. He was skimming through the paper, but when he got to the advertisements in the back he stopped browsing and started reading.

An ad had caught his attention. It was a full-page spread for a strip club called The Velvet Glove on Flagler Street. "Appearing all this week – Climaxxx Films Superstar Monica Foxx" read the copy. There was also an accompanying picture of the headliner, who bore an amazing resemblance to Jennifer Brinkman. That would be his next stop.

Not exactly on the street, but close enough, he thought.

Nick tucked the newspaper away and looked up just in time to see a somewhat familiar face enter the restaurant. Bones McCoy – all 6 foot 3 of him. Nick saw why he was working undercover for the DEA – McCoy was big, bald, and looked like he could wrestle a locomotive. He was obviously on assignment, because he sported at least a week's worth of beard, which complemented his worn jeans and soiled shirt. The gold spike in his left ear was a nice touch.

He spotted Nick and came over to sit down, raising eyebrows of the other diners along the way. The two men shook hands, and Nick ordered his friend a cup of coffee.

"Man, I sure was surprised to hear from you," McCoy began. "I thought you quit the racket."

"I did," Nick replied, "but I got homesick to see that pretty face of yours."

"Get outta here," McCoy said, laughing.

"What are you doing for the DEA?" Nick asked.

"Big sting operation in Atlanta," McCoy answered. "Been workin' the streets there about three months, gettin' tight with the Colombians. But that ain't why you beeped."

"No," Nick answered, "it ain't. You still tight with The Agency?"

"Tight enough to know when to stay away. Why?"

"Someone at Langley sent my personnel file to some big-ass newspaper publisher down here. Guy says he's preparing an exposé on The Agency, and he's putting heat on me for reasons unknown."

"What kind of heat could anyone put on Lucky Nick Seven?"

"Oh, let's see – having me followed, trying to get me to investigate a bogus blackmail scheme, sending a reporter into my place undercover to dig up dirt, threatening to publish everything he knows about me – that kind of stuff. This guy's got clout, too. Do you remember Felicia Hagens?"

McCoy let out a low wolf whistle.

"Do I ever!" he replied. "Whatever happened to her, anyway?"

"She's staying with me on Key Largo," Nick replied.

McCoy chuckled.

"That's why we always called you Lucky Nick," he said.

"Anyway," Nick continued, "this newspaper guy even sent the INS out to hassle her."

McCoy shook his head in amazement.

"Man, when you step in it, you get it all over you," he

said. "This badass got a name?"

"Paul Brinkman."

"Like I said, you get it all over you," McCoy said. "Even I heard of Brinkman. That's one fat cat you don't want to screw with."

"Too late," Nick said. "Before you went underground, did you hear any rumblings at headquarters that might interest me?"

"Only that Currey was extremely pissed about what happened in London," McCoy answered. "You know, Brodie's killing. The Old Man really had to do a tap dance on Capitol Hill. Even did an internal investigation. The suits in the White House threatened to boot his fat ass out of there if he didn't come up with some answers about that and all those terrorist attacks."

"Did he?"

"Not the ones they wanted. He's still under the microscope, and sweating bullets."

"You think he's behind this?"

"Could be. One thing I remember was that he kept asking anyone and everyone in the London office where you were when Brodie bought it. Hey, Nick —" McCoy started to say, then stopped.

Nick slowly shook his head 'no.'

"Best you don't know, pal," Nick said, "so don't ask, and I won't have to lie to you."

McCoy slowly nodded his head knowingly.

"I get ya," he said. "You want me to dig around, see what I can find out?"

"If you can. You know where to reach me if you come up with anything juicy."

The two men got up to leave, Nick left money for the bill, and they walked outside, shaking hands again. Nick offered McCoy a ride back to the airport, but the agent hailed a cab, trying to keep his cover intact.

Nick drove over to The Velvet Glove. Even at 2:30 in the afternoon, the place was jumping. The sounds of loud rock music came from within. Nick paid the $10.00 cover charge and went inside. He went up to the bar and asked the barmaid when Monica Foxx would be on.

"Just finished her set," the barmaid answered, practically shouting to be heard over the music. "Won't be back on for another hour."

Nick thanked her, and wandered around the large room. He watched as one of the "dancers" finished her number on the runway, then went through a curtain against the far wall. Nick figured that's where the dressing rooms had to be, so that's where he went. He also wondered how these girls kept from catching pneumonia.

Nick walked through the entry curtain backstage. He was immediately approached by a very large man, who demanded to know what Nick was doing back there.

"Looking for the men's room," Nick answered, peering around.

He found a door with the name Monica Foxx on it, and started to walk towards it. He got about two steps when the bouncer stepped in front of him, and slammed his open right palm into Nick's chest to stop him. The guy was probably 6 feet 2, 250 pounds, with tattoos everywhere, and a shaved head.

"The can's out front," he snarled, "and the girls don't take no visitors."

"My mistake," Nick said, and turned to walk away. As he did, he could hear the bouncer following him.

Nick put three feet of space between them, then suddenly whirled around, raised his right leg, and delivered a full hard kick to the bouncer's lower abdomen, knocking the wind out of him, causing him to double over in pain. Nick brought him to the floor with an on-target karate chop to the back of the man's neck. Before the guy could regain his senses, Nick grabbed him by the back of his muscle shirt, dragged him to a nearby closet and shoved him inside, closing and locking the door. He then proceeded to Monica Foxx's dressing room.

He knocked on the door but didn't wait for an invitation to come in. Abruptly opening the door, Nick found the girl in the throes of faked passion with a man on the couch. The guy, who looked like an accountant, suddenly jumped up in surprise, and hurriedly pulled on his pants.

"Who – who are you?" he stammered.

"The lady's husband," Nick said. "Get lost."

The man quickly left, and Nick closed the door after him. He leaned against the door, folded his arms across his chest and looked at the girl.

"Jennifer Brinkman, I presume?" he asked.

She didn't answer at first, instead looked at the door, waiting for someone to come to her rescue.

"Don't worry, we won't be disturbed," Nick said. "Schwarzenegger's taking a nap."

"OK," she said. "So you found out. What do you want?"

"Who put you up to this?" Nick demanded.

"What makes you think anybody put me up to anything?" the girl responded.

"Because something like this takes brains, and that's not the part of your body that gets the most workout."

"OK," she replied. "It was Brinkman's idea. He had me come to see you, posing as his daughter. He told me to make you believe I was being blackmailed."

"You missed your calling as an actress," Nick said. "I almost believed your performance. But why me?"

The girl shrugged her shoulders.

"I don't know," she answered. "He just said he needed someone to get close to you, to see what I could find out about you. Look, when The Boss yells, you jump."

"What do you mean, 'The Boss'?"

"Didn't you know? Brinkman owns this place."

"What else does he have a piece of, besides you?"

"I think he owns part of Climaxxx Films, too," the girl replied.

"Damn!" Nick exclaimed. "So that tape you gave me was really one of your feature films?"

She nodded yes.

"But on that tape you looked drugged," Nick said.

"I always get high before a scene," the girl said. "Makes it look more realistic. Look, Mr. Seven, I didn't really do anything wrong, and nobody got hurt. Besides, Brinkman gave me a lot of money to hustle you."

"I'm sure it was worth every penny. What about that name you gave me, Carl Lonergan? What's his connection to this?"

"Brinkman gave me that name. He said Lonergan was on the list of people who sold home videos to Climaxxx."

Nick turned around to leave.

"Hey," the girl said, stopping him.

Nick turned around to look at her.

"Was I really convincing when I came to see you the first time?" she asked in all sincerity.

"Yes, you were," Nick answered, giving her a small smile. "You ought to try acting without being buzzed sometime. Like I said, you missed your calling."

- *Eleven* -

Nick drove to Harry Trent's office on Indianola Avenue. Maybe Trent could tell him if Brinkman's numerous holdings included a certain adult film distributor in San Francisco.

Nick opened the door to Trent Productions and stepped inside, stopping for a moment. The silence was deafening. When he was there the day before, the office was abuzz with activity. Now, there was nobody there. Nick soon saw why.

The place looked like a hurricane had been through. Filing cabinets were overturned, film and video tapes cluttered the floor, and there were papers scattered everywhere. Nick cautiously weeded his way back to Trent's office, calling out his name. No answer.

Harry Trent was lying on the floor behind his desk, the cord from his phone wrapped tightly around his neck. Nick sighed, and slowly shook his head in sorrow. He leaned down and checked Trent's neck for a pulse. As he suspected, the would-be movie mogul wouldn't be producing that remake of "Gone With The Wind" anytime soon.

Nick stood up, and looked around. He thought about searching for the information he came for, but where would he start? The office was a disaster area. As he looked around, one thing caught his eye. There, on the floor next to Trent's body, was a box of matches, decorated in red and blue. Nick picked them up.

"Calhoun's on the Marina, Key Largo, Florida. Reservations suggested."

Cute, boys, he thought, *real cute.*

He put the matches in his pocket and left the office, closing the door behind him, taking the time to wipe his fingerprints off the doorknob. Nick took the stairs down to the basement level, and found a backdoor that emptied into an alley behind the old building. He walked to the street, found a phone booth about midway down the block, and dialed 911. When the operator answered, Nick changed the pitch of his voice and spoke with as close to a Cuban accent as he could.

"Man, you got to come quick! There's a dead guy over here!"

"Sir, may I have your name?" the operator asked.

"Didn't you hear me? There's a dead guy over here! 1165 Indianola! Second floor! Hurry, man!"

"Sir, I need your –"

Nick hung up the phone, and calmly walked back to his car. He got in, lit a cigarette, and watched as a Metro Dade police car pulled up in front of the building a few minutes later. It was the least he could do for his old friend.

Nick drove back to Key Largo, fighting the rush-hour traffic of late afternoon in Miami. It was nearly 6:00 when he pulled the Mustang into the parking lot. As he entered the front door of Calhoun's, he saw Raul, anxiously pacing the floor. When he saw Nick, Raul rushed over to him. Nick could tell something was wrong.

"What is it?" he asked.

Raul motioned his head towards the restaurant.

"Fuzz," he answered.

"The Feds again?" Nick asked.

"No," he answered. "The Locals this time."

Nick went inside and saw Sheriff Ted Cain sitting at the bar. He approached the Sheriff, and extended his right hand. Cain got up from his seat and shook hands with Nick, who was all smiles.

"Well, Sheriff," Nick began, "what can I do for you?"

"Is there someplace private where we can talk?" Cain asked.

Nick ushered him into his office, and closed the door. The two men sat down.

"So," Nick began, "you want my endorsement? I'm flattered."

Cain looked at Nick for a moment.

"We've had a complaint about you, Nick," he said.

"What?" Nick asked, jokingly. "I forget to pay a parking ticket?"

Cain shook his head.

"Something more serious," he said. "Young lady says she was given a doctored drink in here last night. Claims she visited your establishment to have a few drinks, and the next thing she knew she was passed out in the back seat of a cab in front of her apartment. You wouldn't know anything about that, would you?"

Nick thought for a moment, and slowly shook his head 'no.'

"No," he said thoughtfully. "I do remember calling a

cab for a young lady who bagged more than her limit last night, though."

"Pretty sauced up, was she?"

"She was in my opinion," Nick answered. "And being a responsible barkeep, I cut her off and suggested she go home and sleep it off."

"Any witnesses?" Cain asked.

"Sure," Nick answered. "My manager Raul, Felicia, and old Mr. Brady, who was really having a nice time with her."

"Old Mr. Brady?" Cain asked in surprise. "But he's gay!"

Nick shrugged his shoulders.

"Maybe he wanted to see if the grass was any greener on the other side before it was too late," Nick answered.

Cain exhaled heavily.

"Look, Nick," he said, "you know I wouldn't be here if this didn't sound legitimate."

"Frankly, Ted," Nick said, "I'm surprised at your sudden selective amnesia."

"What selective amnesia?"

"Don't you remember what happened last year?" Nick asked. "You know, when your son came in here with some of his buddies and got loaded? I didn't let him drink anymore because he'd had too much, and I did the same for that girl last night. In fact, if memory serves, I even drove junior home – personally – because I knew if he got on the road in his condition, he'd either kill himself or somebody else."

Cain paused for a moment.

"Of course I remember," he finally said. "And I also

remember that you kept it out of the papers. Nick, what connection do you have with Paul Brinkman?"

"Oh," Nick said, "him again. Is he the one who sent you here?" Cain said nothing, so Nick continued. "Let me guess: the young lady from last night just happens to work for Brinkman. Am I warm?"

"Scorched," Cain answered. "Brinkman's the one who filed the complaint. I didn't put much stock in it, but I had to check it out anyway."

"So why does the High Sheriff come down to check out a simple drunk and disorderly? I thought that's why you had Deputies."

"Ordinarily you'd be right," Cain answered. "But this is an election year, and a man like Brinkman buys a lot of muscle with his money."

"Can you keep him off my ass for a little while?" Nick asked.

"Yeah," Cain said, rising and putting on his hat, "I think so. Just don't stick your hand in the cage."

Cain left, and Nick returned to the bar.

"What happened?" Raul asked anxiously.

"As we suspected," Nick answered, "our floozy from last night is in the employ of a certain newspaper publisher."

While Nick was bantering with the Sheriff, Felicia was busy doing her own investigation. She had put on some old clothes, wrapped a bandanna around her woven hair and went to Brinkman's office building in Miami. Going to the service entrance, she saw three people from the janitorial service that was contracted to clean the offices and joined them as they entered the building.

Felicia found a trash receptacle on wheels and pushed it into one of the elevators with another custodian. She took the elevator to the second-highest floor and proceeded to go from office to office, emptying wastebaskets. After an hour of blending in, she took the elevator to the penthouse floor. As the elevator doors opened, Felicia cautiously peeked into the hallway. Seeing nobody on the floor, she exited the elevator and proceeded to Brinkman's office suite.

Felicia checked the doorframe for security devices. Finding none, she knelt down, took her own burglar's tool from her pocket and proceeded to unlock the door. Once inside the massive office, she hesitated, looking around the room for motion detectors. She found one on the far side of the room, near a large credenza. Felicia presumed that was where Brinkman kept his most valuable files.

She went instead to Brinkman's desk. As she suspected, all of the drawers were locked. Felicia took a penlight from her pocket and shone its light over the top of the desk. She spied Brinkman's calender. Flipping through the pages for the previous week yielded nothing more than the usual meetings and lunch dates, but one entry for the following day caught her eye: "Call DC." She also found a switch under the desk with wires leading to the video camera behind the plush leather chair and the decorative paperweight positioned in front of the guest chairs.

Finding nothing else of interest, Felicia left the office, locking the door behind her. She took the elevator down to the service entrance and left the building, removing the bandanna and fluffing her hair with her fingers. She drove back to Calhoun's.

Nick was waiting for her at his table. Felicia leaned over and kissed him before sitting down.

"How did it go?" he asked.

"In and out, no problem," she replied. "I found –"

"Wait," Nick interrupted. "Let's go home. You can tell me there."

They drove back to Nick's condo. When they were inside, he poured two glasses of wine, which they took out to the deck overlooking the water. When they were seated in the moonlight, Nick fired up a cigarette.

It was a cool night for Southern Florida, and a gentle breeze was blowing, bringing in the smell of salt air from the ocean. The wind chimes hanging near the deck played softly. Nick lit a candle on the table, and relaxed in his chair.

"So what did you find?" Nick asked.

"Not much," Felicia answered. "Everything was locked up. There's a microphone hidden on the desk in a paperweight, and a camera behind the desk. The only other thing I saw was a note on his calender for tomorrow: 'Call DC.' Mean anything?"

Nick thought for a minute.

"Probably someone's initials," he said, "or a nickname. Could be Washington, D.C."

"What did you find out today?" she asked.

Nick recounted the events of his day, including Trent's murder and his visit from the Sheriff.

"Poor Harry, " Felicia said, shaking her head. "So that bimbo last night was on Brinkman's pad?"

"Looks that way."

"And the cheerleader works for him, too?"

Nick took a sip of wine before answering.

"Yeah," he replied. "The whole blackmail thing was made up. Brinkman sent her here to get close to me, probably hoping I'd say or do something he could use against me."

"And just so you'd give him info for some article he wants to write?" Felicia asked, a tone of disbelief in her voice.

"That's the part that doesn't make sense," Nick replied. "Someone with a large media organization at their disposal doesn't need a guy like me who's been out of circulation for five years to supply gossip. Hell, I know at least a dozen people working at headquarters right now who'd take the money and talk, no questions asked."

They both sat in silence for a few minutes, thinking.

"You think Old Lard Butt is behind this?" Felicia finally asked, referring to their former boss at The Agency.

"Could be," Nick answered. "According to Bones, he was really interested in my whereabouts the night Brodie was killed. I just can't figure who would want to kill Harry Trent, though. He was no threat. Or why Brinkman has my butt in his gunsight."

"Maybe he's on The Agency's payroll," Felicia said, off-handedly. "Maybe he just has a thing for porno actresses."

Nick suddenly sat up straight in his chair, and looked at her.

"Say that again," he said.

"Maybe he has a thing for porno actresses?" Felicia

repeated quizzically.

"No, no," Nick said. "The first part."

"Maybe Brinkman's on The Agency's payroll?"

Nick snapped his fingers.

"That has to be it!" he said. "I'll bet if I checked out Brinkman's background I'd find a few skeletons that he'd want to keep hidden, too."

"But why would The Agency wait all this time to come after you?"

"Closure," Nick answered. "Bones said The Old Man had to do some fast talking to explain what happened in London. And I think I know why he's pressuring me."

"Why?"

Nick paused for a moment, not sure if he should say anything more. Finally, he decided that if he couldn't trust her now, he never could.

"There's something I didn't tell you when I came back from London," he started. "I was wired for sound when I confronted Brodie in that alley, and I got his whole confession on tape. He was behind all those supposed terrorist attacks that they credited to Lavender."

Felicia slowly shook her head in amazement.

"Wow," she finally said. "Does Currey know about it?"

"I sent word to him that I had something embarrassing, and that I'd leak it if he contacted either one of us again."

"So where is it?"

"Someplace safe," Nick answered. "But maybe not safe enough. Is your brother still manager of that bank in Barbados, and can you trust him?"

"Yeah," Felicia said. "Why?"

"Tomorrow, I'm going to give you a package to mail to

him, with instructions to put it in a safe deposit box for me. I want you to call him, from a payphone, to let him know it's on its way, and tell him not to open it, just deposit it for me. Will he do that?"

"Of course," Felicia said. "He my little brother, and he knows if he don't do what I say, I'll kick his ass."

The next morning, Nick took the wristwatch recorder he wore in London when he killed Brodie, made a copy of it onto a micro-cassette and packaged it, along with all the photos and files he had on floppy discs from the operation. He addressed it to the bank in Barbados and gave it to Felicia to mail for him, instructing her to be careful not to be followed on her way to the Post Office. As Felicia left the condo, Nick noticed a manilla envelope outside the front door. He took it inside, opened it, and discovered some photographs.

They were taken with a digital camera, with the times and date from the day before visible in the lower left corner. There were pictures of Nick outside The Florentine with Bones McCoy, Nick entering then leaving The Velvet Glove, Nick leaving Harry Trent's building right after he discovered the body, Nick and Felicia leaving Calhoun's, even Nick and Felicia sitting on the deck of the condo.

Where are the ones from the bedroom after we came inside? Nick thought.

He put the pictures back in the envelope, and locked them in the safe in his den. Nick sat down at his desk and leaned back, rocking in his swivel chair. He took a sip of coffee and lit a cigarette. Nick had to give Brinkman credit – he really knew how to push someone's buttons.

First the bogus blackmail story, then the girl in the bar, now a day in the life of Nick Seven told in pictures. The Big Man knew how to throw his weight around, too, if all it took was a phone call to arrange a visit from the Immigration service and the local law authorities. No wonder he was such an expert at engineering leveraged buyouts. Nick wondered if Brinkman's pockets were deep enough to hire someone to kill Harry Trent. He also wondered what the hell it was Brinkman really wanted from him, and what other surprises the tycoon had planned.

Just then, the front doorbell rang. Nick opened it to see two men in suits standing there, flashing police badges.

"Mr. Seven?" one of them asked.

"Yeah," Nick replied, "I'm Nick Seven."

"Metro Dade Police," one of them said. "I'm Detective Carson, this is my partner, Detective Blades. May we come in?"

"Can I stop you?" Nick asked rhetorically as he held the door open.

"Mr. Seven," Detective Carson began, "do you know a man named Harry Trent?"

"Yeah," Nick replied, "Harry's an old friend. Is he in trouble?"

The Detectives paused a moment.

"He's dead," Detective Blades said.

Nick said nothing.

"You don't seem too surprised," Blades continued.

"I knew the business Harry was in," Nick explained. "Some of his customers played rough."

"Just what is your connection with the late Mr. Trent?"

Carson asked.

"As I said," Nick replied, "he is – was – an old friend. We did some business together a few years ago."

"What kind of business?" Carson asked.

"I'd rather not say," Nick answered.

"Maybe you'd feel more like talking at Police Headquarters," Blades interjected.

"No," Nick said, "I don't think that would make me feel more conversational. Perhaps I should explain. I'm a former employee of the United States Government, and Harry Trent used to do some work for me."

"What branch of the Government are you a former employee of?" Carson asked.

Nick paused for a moment.

"Central Intelligence Agency," he finally answered.

"And Trent was one of your snitches?" Blades asked.

"Something like that," Nick answered.

"We have a description of a man seen leaving Trent's office building yesterday about the time he was killed," Carson said. "From the description, the man looks a lot like you."

"So do half the men in Miami," Nick responded. "Guess I must have common features. What brought you all the way down here to my door?"

"Then you wouldn't mind coming in for a line-up?" Carson asked, ignoring Nick's question.

Nick looked at the detective through narrowed eyes.

"Got a warrant?" Nick asked.

Carson looked down at the floor.

"Look, fellas," Nick continued, "I'd love to help you, but I honestly don't know who would want to kill Harry

Trent. As I said, he was in a rough trade with rough people."

"Then you haven't seen him lately?" Blades pressed.

"I didn't say that," Nick said. "I saw Harry a couple of days ago."

"On what business?" Carson asked.

"Personal business," Nick answered. "Any law being broken when a man stops in to say hi to an old friend?"

"No," Carson answered. "Nice place you have here. Mind if we look around?"

"Say, about that warrant–" Nick started to say.

Carson and Blades looked at each other.

"OK, Mr. Seven," Blades said. "We'll be on our way. If you think of anything that might help, call us at this number."

He handed Nick a business card, and the two cops left. As they went out the front door, Felicia was coming in.

"More heat?" she asked as Nick closed and locked the door.

"Yeah," Nick answered. "Miami Police, asking questions about Trent's murder. Said they got a description of a guy who looks like me leaving the scene right after Harry's demise. I can guess who gave them my name and address."

"What we do now?" Felicia asked.

Nick thought for a minute.

"I think it's a great day to take the boat out," he answered.

"Take the boat out?" she responded in surprise. "Where to?"

"Oh, I don't know," Nick answered. "Out there

somewhere, maybe up the coast a little ways towards Palm Beach. I hear Paul Brinkman has an estate that overlooks the ocean."

- *Twelve* -

It was a beautiful day for a cruise. The temperature was a pleasant 72 degrees, the blue of the sky was punctuated by a few puffy white clouds, and there was a breeze blowing. Nick piloted the Bayliner up the Southern Florida coast, past Miami Beach. An hour and a half later they had reached the inter-coastal waterway near Singer Island on Palm Beach Shores.

Felicia had made herself at home, wearing a bikini that showed off to full advantage her bronzed supermodel physique. As she lay on the deck catching some sun, Nick kept an eye out for the home he was looking for. There was a lot of money sitting on these shores, old money, the kind made by previous generations and squandered by the new ones. Finally, he found the one he sought, and slowed the engine down. Nick cruised a few hundred yards off the shore until he found a spot that showed off the house. He stopped the boat, and dropped anchor.

Felicia got up from the deck and went into the cabin, bringing out a large take-out bag from Calhoun's. Nick had called the club and had them prepare lunch for them to take on the trip, specifically telling Raul to include a couple of bottles of their best wine. As she set up lunch on the deck, Nick brought his camera out from the cabin. He put a 300mm lense on the camera, focused on the house, and took a few shots. There was nothing much to see – yet. But he could wait. He was good at waiting. He'd made a career out of waiting for his prey to show itself.

They sat down to lunch, and enjoyed the warm sun and cool breeze. Nick looked at Felicia, and couldn't help but appreciate her incredible beauty. He just couldn't take his eyes off of her. Other men would probably kill to trade places with him for one night. Maybe Bones McCoy was right, after all – maybe he really *was* "Lucky Nick Seven."

Felicia caught Nick staring at her, and furrowed her brow.

"What you lookin' at?" she demanded.

Nick grinned.

"Just the prettiest girl that ever walked into my life," he answered.

"Who?" she asked in mock surprise, then laughed.

Nick laughed along with her, then opened a bottle of White Zinfandel. He poured them each a glass, and handed one to Felicia, stopping to toast to her by raising his glass.

"Any regrets?" he asked.

"About what?"

"Leaving your family in Barbados, coming up here, taking up with an over-the-hill hired gun, that kind of stuff," he answered.

"Who you callin' over-the-hill?" she asked. "No, Hon, no regrets – except one."

"Which one is that?"

She got up and came over to Nick, sitting on his lap. She wrapped her arms around him, and gave him a passionate kiss.

"That I didn't do it sooner," she answered.

"Small world," he managed to say.

Felicia stood up and slipped out of her bikini top, giving her size 38 breasts their freedom. She stretched her arms back, pushing her chest forward slightly to give Nick the full view.

"Sure is gettin' hot out here in the sun," she said lazily. "Think it's any cooler down below?"

Nick admired her well-toned body.

"Why don't we go down and find out?" he replied, standing up. Nick grabbed the bottle of wine as they went below decks to the cabin.

Must be something about this sea air, he thought.

Felicia continued to make herself comfortable by quickly peeling off the bottom half of her bikini. She lay down on the bed in the cabin and reclined seductively, pulling one leg towards her body. Nick was pulling his shirt over his head when Felicia gave out a low wolf whistle.

"Hey, sailor," she teased. "Lookin' for a good time?"

Nick slipped out of the rest of his clothes and joined her on the bed.

"Sure," he replied, playing along. "Know where I can find one?"

She playfully smacked his arm.

"That's not helpin' to set the mood," she said.

"Maybe this will," he replied, taking her in his arms.

Nick began kissing Felicia as she ran her hands along his muscled torso. He responded by gently fondling her breasts as Felicia slid her tongue deep into Nick's mouth.

She proceeded to nuzzle his neck with her soft, full lips.

"Mmm," she said. "You smell nice."

"So do you," Nick replied. "Don't ever change that perfume."

Felicia chuckled seductively.

"That turn you on, Tough Guy?" she teased while moving her hand below his waist, fondling him.

"That's not all," he whispered in her ear.

Felicia lay down on her back, pulling Nick with her. The ocean's waves were rocking the boat as Nick resumed kissing her. Felicia reached down and took ahold of Nick's erection, guiding it into her body. He began rhythmically making love to her. Felicia picked up his rhythm and moved with him, becoming more aroused.

Nick wrapped his arms around Felicia, kissing her ravenously on her mouth and neck. She pulled her legs up further, wrapping them around Nick's waist, forcing him to plunge deeper into her tight body. He was getting more aroused and increased the speed of his movements. Felicia moaned in pleasure. Nick cried out softly as he climaxed deep inside Felicia's body. She cried out louder as she experienced her own pleasure.

After catching his breath, Nick gently withdrew from Felicia and lay next to her. They were both perspiring from the heat of their passions and panting softly. Felicia placed her head on Nick's shoulder and closed her eyes while running her fingertips over his chest.

"You all right?" he softly asked.

"Like I said," she whispered. "No regrets."

They both drifted off into a light sleep, helped by the tide gently moving the boat in place. After an hour of resting, Nick awoke and glanced at his watch, noting that it was almost 5:30. He quietly slipped out of bed as Felicia dozed contentedly. Nick got dressed and climbed the steps to the deck to see if there was anything happening on shore.

The sunset had started to put on its nightly show when Nick emerged from the cabin. He picked up the camera, and took another look at Brinkman's estate. This time there was some activity going on in the massive backyard that butted up to the beach. Nick crouched down, and looked at the faces of the people sitting in the gazebo. There were three men, each holding a cocktail. He recognized Brinkman, but the other two faces were shielded by shadows. Nick cursed softly to himself, and hoped they would come out so he could see who Brinkman was having over for dinner.

He waited a full twenty minutes. Finally, the three men stood up, and exited the gazebo. Nick started taking pictures as they walked down the three steps into the backyard, and into what was left of the daylight. One of the men was older, portly, with thinning gray hair. His back was to the ocean, so Nick couldn't see his face. The other man was visible, so Nick took his picture, even though he didn't recognize him.

Brinkman turned towards the ocean, and waved his hand in a sweeping motion across the beach, as though he were showing off the expanse of real estate that he and he alone possessed. Finally, the third man turned around to admire the view, and Nick got a look at his face.

"Son of a bitch!" he softly exclaimed.

Nick took as many shots as he could before the men

turned back towards the mansion, and went inside. Felicia came up from the cabin, pulling a t-shirt over her head, having put on a pair of cut-off jean shorts and sandals.

"What is it, Hon?" she asked, crouching down next to Nick.

Nick stared at Brinkman's estate a moment before answering.

"It's time for me to raise the stakes," he replied.

It was almost 8:30 when Nick pulled into his dock at the yacht club. He was tying up the boat, and Felicia was getting their stuff from the cabin when Nick heard the patter of feet running towards the boat. It was Raul.

"Chief!" he called out. "You better come inside – quick!"

"What's wrong?" Nick asked.

"Plenty trouble!" Raul exclaimed as he ran back towards Calhoun's.

Nick and Felicia ran after him to see what was going on. As they approached the restaurant, Nick could hear raised voices coming from inside, followed by the sound of breaking glass.

They ran into the bar and saw a fight in full bloom between six burly men. The other patrons were taking cover behind tables and running towards the exit. Nick ran into his office as Felicia jumped into the fray, attempting to pull two of the men off each other. She got thrown halfway across the room for her trouble, landing on a table that fell to the floor under the impact. Felicia regained her senses and quickly got back on her feet.

Now that she was mad, Felicia went after the same two men, separating them, pinning one of them against the bar.

His five buddies converged on her with raised fists, one of them brandishing a broken beer bottle, which he had poised in the air, ready to strike. Three of the men had turned Felicia around, and were holding her against the bar. She struggled, but couldn't break free. She glanced up and saw the sharp edges of the broken glass, as the man holding it prepared to bring it in contact with her face.

The screaming of the crowd and yelling of the six men was instantly stilled by the sound of a gunshot. The men stopped, turned around, and saw Nick standing atop one of the tables, his 9mm Beretta in his right hand, and a double-barreled shotgun in his left, both pointed at them.

"Let the girl go!" he ordered.

No one made a move, so Nick took aim and fired a shot from the Beretta. It went dangerously close to the ear of one of the men, shattering a bottle of liquor on the barback.

"Now!" he barked.

The men let Felicia go, and she hurried to Nick's side. He handed her the shotgun, which she pointed at the men.

"Raul, call the Sheriff," Nick ordered.

When he said that, one of the men tried to make a run for the door, but Felicia jumped in front of him, giving him a good look down both barrels of the shotgun.

"Be a shame to rearrange that pretty face, man," she angrily said.

The thug raised his hands and went back to the bar.

"Is anybody hurt?" Nick called out to the customers. Hearing nothing but confused mumbling, he addressed the men. "Who started this?"

No one answered, so Nick jumped down from the table and approached the group. He went up to the biggest man, the one who was about to hit Felicia with the broken bottle. Nick had a full rage going and a look of total anger on his face.

"You," Nick said, grabbing the guy by the collar and dragging him towards the front door. "Let's you and me go outside for a chat. Felicia, watch the others until the cops get here."

Nick dragged the guy outside, and around to the side of the building, where he threw him into a row of trash cans. He pointed the Beretta at the man's face.

"Who sent you assholes here?" Nick demanded.

The man said nothing, so Nick picked him up by the front of his shirt, and dragged him over to the edge of the marina, keeping his gun pointed at him the whole time. He turned the man around, his back to the water, his heels on the edge of the dock, and leaned him over the water. The man gasped.

"Can you swim?" Nick asked, holding his gun at the man's head.

The man shook his head in a vehement "no".

"You'd better learn fast. Now, one more time: who sent you?"

Still no response, so Nick lowered the man closer to the water. The look of fear on the man's face got more intense. Nick never knew a man's eyes could open that wide.

"We just wanted a few brews to blow off some steam after work," he managed to say.

"Wrong answer," Nick said, as he let his grip on the

man's shirt slip a little. "My arm's getting tired. I don't know how much longer I can hold onto you. Wanna try again?"

"OK, OK," he stammered. "Guy at work gave us each a hundred to come in and bust up your place."

"Where do you work?"

"Truck drivers," he gasped.

"For who?" Nick demanded, getting annoyed.

"Brinkman Publishing," the man exclaimed. "We're Teamsters."

Nick took in the answer, cursing Brinkman in his head.

"You gonna let me up now?" the man pleaded. "I told ya I can't swim!"

"Tough shit," Nick said, letting go of the man's shirt, dropping him into the water five feet below where he landed with a loud splash.

The man was floundering in the water, calling out for help when Sheriff Ted Cain ran up to Nick.

"What happened?" Cain demanded.

"I don't know, Ted," Nick calmly answered. "Poor bastard must have slipped and fallen in. Somebody should fish him out."

Nick tucked his gun into the waistband of his pants and walked back into what was left of Calhoun's to survey the damage and placate his clientele. As people were leaving, Nick spoke to as many as he could, apologizing for the fracas, and hoping most of them would come back. The Sheriff's Deputies had all of the men in handcuffs and were herding them outside. Two more deputies were busy taking statements from Raul and some of the customers. Nick found Felicia.

"Are you OK?" he asked.

"Yeah," she said. "Just a little sore. Ain't seen a fight like that since I left home!"

"And STILL no regrets?"

That made her laugh, as she collapsed on Nick's arm, which he wrapped around her.

"Come on," he said, "I need a drink."

As he reached behind the bar for a bottle of Scotch and two glasses, he looked around the room at the broken furniture and glass.

"My insurance man is going to love this," he said as they went into his office.

They sat down and Nick poured them each a healthy shot. There was a knock on the door, and Ted Cain entered the room. Nick offered him a seat and a drink. The Sheriff took the seat.

"Who were those guys, Nick?" he asked.

"Beats me," Nick answered. "We just got back from a day on the water and there was this Pier 6 brawl going on."

"Did the one outside tell you anything?"

"Only that they were Teamsters looking to blow off a little steam after work."

"Nothing else?" Cain queried.

"Like what?" Nick responded.

"Like who they work for?"

"You can find that out easy enough," Nick said. "Why are you leaning on me, anyway? I'm the injured party here, remember? What's going on, Ted?"

Cain paused for a moment, looking down at the floor.

"I had a call from a Detective Carson with the Miami

Dade Metro Squad this afternoon," Cain continued. "Says he came calling on you this morning about a homicide they're investigating up there, and that you weren't very cooperative."

"I told those guys what I knew," Nick answered. "They asked me if I knew Harry Trent, I told them I did. They asked me if I knew who killed him, I told them I didn't. That's it and that's all."

"He also said you fit the description of a man seen leaving Trent's building about the time of his murder."

"What can I say?" Nick said. "I've got a common-looking face. And being the sharp investigator you are, doesn't it strike you as odd that out of all the people in southern Florida, those two cops got my name and address?"

"Are you saying Brinkman sent them here?" Cain asked.

"Yes, that's what I'm saying," Nick replied.

Cain looked down again before responding.

"Look, Nick," he said, "if you're withholding evidence in a homicide, you won't have to worry about Brinkman coming after you – he'll have the Police do it for him, and there won't be a damn thing I can do about it."

"Ted, I swear," Nick said. "If I find out anything, you'll be the first one I call."

Cain shook his head and smirked.

"You're full of shit," he said, standing up and leaving the room.

"Did that guy outside really tell you anything?" Felicia asked after the door was closed.

"Yeah," Nick said. "He and his buddies work for

Brinkman Publishing."

"Son of a bitch!" she exclaimed.

"Let's get the hell out of here," Nick said, as they left the office.

Things had started to settle down in the bar. The Deputies and customers had departed. Nick told Raul to send everyone home and lock up, and that they'd clean up the place tomorrow. He and Felicia got into Nick's car and drove home.

A little later, Nick was watching the news, nursing a drink.

"This breaking story just in from Atlanta," the anchorwoman said. "Drug Enforcement Agency authorities report having made the arrests tonight of four Colombian drug lords, and confiscating nearly 1,000 pounds of cocaine. Officials said this was the result of a months-long undercover sting operation between several Government Law Enforcement agencies, and that the cocaine represents one of the largest amounts ever seized. Now, turning to Sports –"

Nick turned off the TV, a satisfied smile on his face.

Way to go, Bones! he thought.

* * *

3:00 A.M. Nick couldn't sleep. Too much on his mind, but one thing in particular.

He looked over at the sleeping beauty next to him. He gazed at Felicia for a long time, thinking about how his life had changed for the better since she was a part of it. He also remembered a promise he'd make to himself to not let anything, or anyone, change that. Nick gently shook her.

"Hey," he said softly. "You awake?"

Felicia scooted up onto the pillows and looked at him through sleepy eyes.

"I am now," she answered. "What's wrong?"

Nick paused for a minute before answering.

"I felt something tonight during that fight in the bar," he softly answered. "Something I haven't felt for a long time – fear."

"That's natural, Hon," she answered. "My juices got goin' again, too."

"I don't mean fear from the fight, or having to take on those dimwits. I've faced down guys tougher than them before. I mean fear of something else."

"What?"

Nick paused again, and finally looked Felicia square in the eyes.

"When I saw those guys going after you, I got scared. More scared than I've been in years."

"You were afraid they were goin' to hurt me?" she asked.

Nick nodded yes. Felicia scooted over closer to him, and put her arm around him.

"You a sweet man," she said. "To tell the truth, I was kinda scared myself."

"Felicia," he said after another pause, trying to collect his thoughts, "I've already lost one person that I thought meant everything in the world to me, and I don't want to lose another one. When I saw that guy about to hit you with that broken bottle, I just went crazy, afraid that you might be taken from me."

She rubbed his back and shoulders.

"Don't worry, Hon," she answered soothingly. "Nobody goin' to take me 'way from you."

"Do you really think it's safe for you to stay here?" he asked. "Maybe you should take a trip back home, at least until this is over."

Felicia stopped caressing Nick and sat up, looking him in the eye this time.

"We had this conversation before, remember?" she said. "You sent me 'way once because you was worried I might get hurt. Well, this time it's different – this is where I want to be, this is where I belong, and this is where I'm stayin'."

Nick started to protest, but Felicia interrupted him.

"That's it and that's all!" she said. "Besides, you need me 'round to pick up after you and stop the bleedin'."

After a moment, they both laughed softly, and Nick slid under the covers. Felicia curled up next to him and began slowly rubbing his chest. Nick put his arm around her naked shoulder and returned her caresses.

"Like I tell you before," she said softly, "you a sweet man, and I'm glad you're lookin' out for me."

Soon they both fell asleep.

* * *

Late the following afternoon, Bones McCoy was back at CIA headquarters. He had received his next assignment from Currey. He was to go to Bogota, Colombia, and help close down the rest of the pipeline he had put a dent in the day before.

Before he could leave the country, he had one thing to check on. McCoy went down to one of the sub-basements to the computer room. He made sure no one was inside, then logged onto the phone records of the agency. All incoming and outgoing calls were tracked and the numbers stored in a database, along with the times of the calls, for security reasons. After a few minutes, McCoy had found what he was looking for, and wrote it down. He logged off of the computer and left the building.

Back on Key Largo, Nick was puttering around the condo. Calhoun's would be closed for at least another day, until the insurance guys sifted through the rubble and haggled over how much they would fork over to settle the claim. All of the staff was enjoying a day off with pay. Nick found himself getting bored, not having the club to go to for action. The phone rang.

"Hey, Goldilocks," a familiar voice on the other end started, "this is Papa Bear. Can you talk?"

It was Bones McCoy.

"Yeah," Nick answered, "go ahead."

"Listen good, my man," McCoy said. "You're in way over your head this time. Dessert Storm was a day at the beach compared to this."

"What did you find out?

Nick listened intently, and wrote down what McCoy said to him.

"Thanks, Bones," Nick said. "I owe you another one. Any advice?"

"Yeah," McCoy said. "Get your ass outta there while you still have it – and don't let anything happen to that pretty lady of yours, or Papa Bear just might come callin'."

"Forget it," Nick responded. "She only goes for good-lookin' guys. Listen, thanks for the info, and take care of yourself. I don't want to read about you in the obituaries, OK?"

"Not a chance," McCoy said, hanging up.

Felicia came into the room as Nick hung up the phone.

"Who was that?" she asked.

"Bones," Nick answered.

"What he have to say?"

Nick approached Felicia and wrapped his arms around her, giving her a kiss.

"He said that if I didn't take good care of you, he would," Nick answered.

"Did you tell him I only go for good-lookin' guys?" she responded.

- *Thirteen* -

It turned out to be another sleepless night for Nick, so he decided to sit on the deck for a while. He broke out a bottle of Grouse from behind the bar, and took it with him. As he sipped the Scotch and smoked, he leaned back and gazed up at the night sky. It was a clear night over the ocean, with a few well-placed stars to accent the darkness. He listened to the waves steadily wash up on the nearby shore. The gentle evening breeze made the wind chimes play softly. Looking out at the horizon, Nick could see the shrimp boats coming back into port, weighted down with tomorrow's fresh catch for the local restaurants. This was where he did his best thinking. What he was thinking about, though, wasn't good. He was remembering something Felicia said the night before – "Nobody's going to take me away from you."

Funny , Nick thought, *but if you put a Scottish accent to it, I've heard those words before.*

Nick took out another cigarette, tapped the butt end on his gold lighter a couple of times, then lit up. He looked at the lighter for a moment before putting it on the table next to his cigarettes. Nick was remembering that was what Gwyn, his late wife, had said, shortly before she was killed in that explosion in Glasgow – with the bomb that was meant for him, not her. He had tried to send her away, too, to someplace safe while he was chasing the elusive Miles Lavender. She was a stubborn gal, though, and refused to budge, no matter how much he argued with her – just like Felicia. He had caved in that time, too, and look where it got him.

Nick looked again at the gold lighter.

Lucky Nick, he thought. *That's what they always called me. Lucky, hell – the only person I'm good luck for is the undertaker. People have a nasty habit of getting dead around me. Gwyn, Sanders, Brodie, Trent – and so many others I can't even remember their damn faces, let alone their names. Maybe that nickname didn't mean good luck for me, but bad luck for everyone else.*

His train of thought was interrupted by the sound of the patio door sliding open, and small feet scuffling across the deck. Felicia, still half asleep and wearing one of Nick's sports shirts that barely covered her curvaceous ass, pulled up a chair and sat down.

"Ya know," she said wearily, "keepin' up with your night time habits ain't helpin' my beauty sleep, Hon."

"Like you need beauty sleep," Nick responded.

She smacked him playfully on the arm.

"Shut up and pour me a drink," she said.

Felicia took a long sip from the glass of Grouse Nick handed her.

"I think you're starting to get civilized," Nick said.

"Why do you say that?" she asked.

"I couldn't help notice that you dressed before coming outside this time," he quipped.

"I didn't want to make the neighbors jealous," she

responded. "What's wrong, Hon?"

Nick took a sip of his drink.

"Tell me something," he said. "Do they still believe in black magic on Barbados?"

"You mean hexes and stuff like that?"

"Yeah."

"No, Hon," she answered. "We stopped believin' in that when we got indoor plumbing. Why?"

"Because I think I'm a jinx," Nick answered.

Felicia laughed out loud.

"OK," she said. "I'll play. Why you think you're a jinx?"

"Because everyone I've ever gotten close to has ended up dead," Nick answered. "First Gwyn, then Brodie, now Trent – plus countless others over the years. The guys in The Agency used to call me 'Lucky Nick,' but I think my luck's running out."

"You still worried 'bout me, aren't you?" she asked rhetorically.

"I just don't want the same thing to happen to you, that's all."

Felicia sipped her drink and set the glass on the table.

"You know what your trouble is?" she asked. "You think too much. You're not a jinx, there's no cloud hangin' over your head, and your luck's not runnin' out. You're just stuck on somethin' you can't figure out, and your mind's runnin' loco because of it. You'll figure this one out, just like you always do."

She stood up and took Nick by the hand.

"Come on," she said. "You need some sleep – and no arguments!"

Nick smiled slyly.

"What if I'm not sleepy?" he asked.

Felicia returned his look.

"Maybe you need some exercise to get you tired," she coyly replied.

"Hmm," Nick mused, "it's too late to go to the gym and work out."

Felicia stood over Nick, straddling his legs, and took ahold of the top button on the shirt she was wearing.

"How 'bout we play a game," she said. "I'll ask a question, and for every right answer, I unfasten a button."

Nick looked her up and down.

"Three buttons, three questions," he said. "OK, I accept your challenge."

"You haven't heard the questions," she teased. "First question: are you crazy 'bout me?"

Nick got a thoughtful look on his face.

"Let's see," he said. "Yes?"

"Right answer," Felicia said, unfastening the first button. "Next question: would you do anythin' for me?"

"I'd have to say yes again."

"Very good," she said, unfastening the second button, giving Nick a full view of her breasts. "You must have played this game before. Last question: any regrets 'bout havin' me here with you?"

Nick looked into her soft brown eyes.

"No," he said.

"Is that your final answer?" she teased, unfastening the last button.

Felicia sat down on Nick's lap, facing him, and wrapped her arms around his neck, rubbing the back of his neck as she kissed him. Nick reached under the shirt, caressing her smooth skin, allowing his hands to linger over her breasts before moving down to her backside, where he slipped his fingers in between Felicia's legs. They continued kissing passionately as Felicia moved one of her hands down to Nick's lap, in response to the sudden rise she felt in his pants.

Deftly unfastening his fly, she freed his burgeoning manhood, and began stroking him. Felicia's scent was driving Nick crazy again. Between that and her soft hands he became instantly erect. Felicia slid her body down further, taking Nick completely inside of her. They continued their passionate kissing. Nick began massaging Felicia's firm buttocks as she rode him while hungrily devouring his mouth, steadily increasing the speed and intensity of her gyrations until they both climaxed.

* * *

The next morning, Nick's mind was more clear. During the night, he had figured an angle that he hadn't thought of before. He picked up the phone and dialed the number for The Washington Post. When the operator answered, he asked to speak with Dave Burke.

Dave Burke was a writer for the Post, and his popular daily column, "Burke's Beat," usually managed to ruffle as many feathers as it did to sell advertising for the paper. Burke always managed to find the seamy underside of Capitol Hill politics, and turned it into fodder for his loyal readers. He had once spent time in jail defending his constitutional rights by not revealing a news source to a

Federal Grand Jury, but this didn't make him any less popular – or controversial. If anyone could find out what Nick wanted to know, it was Burke. They had become friends when Nick was with the CIA and Burke needed a favor, and Nick had always admired his guts for not buckling under to the Grand Jury. Now, it was Nick's turn to ask.

They chatted for a few minutes, and made a date to meet later that day.

Nick caught a commuter out of Miami, arriving at Washington National around noon, then took a cab to Duke Ziebert's restaurant. He occupied a booth, ordered coffee, lit a cigarette, and waited for Dave Burke. Burke came in a few minutes later and saw Nick. They shook hands, and Burke sat down, a broad smile on his face.

"Nick Seven," Burke enthusiastically stated. "The last guy I expected to get a call from. Where the hell have you been hiding?"

"Key Largo," Nick answered. "Been there since I quit The Agency a few years ago."

"Finally found the good life, eh?" Burke said.

"It was until recently," Nick responded.

"Why?" Burke asked, his reporter's instinct coming to the surface. "Is there trouble in paradise?"

"Yeah," Nick answered. "That's why I called. I need your help, Dave."

Burke eyed Nick suspiciously.

"What do I get out of this?" he asked, warily.

Nick chuckled softly.

"Same old Dave Burke," he said. "Unless my memory is failing, you still owe me a favor or two from before."

Burke slowly nodded his head in agreement.

"So I do," he replied. "But if you're asking me to dig up anything risky –"

"Worry not," Nick replied, "I'll make it worth your trouble."

"So shoot," Dave said. "What do you need?"

"Ever hear of Paul Brinkman?" Nick asked.

"Who hasn't?" he asked rhetorically. "Everybody in our business knows Brinkman. He's in a class all by himself. He even got his picture in Who Screwed Who in America. Is the big man giving you the blues?"

"Something like that," Nick answered. "I need to know whatever there is to know about him. You know – background, military record, how he got the money to build that empire of his, the whole package."

"So why ask me?"

"Because you're in a class all by *your*self," Nick answered. "You know everything about everybody."

Burke held up his hands and laughed.

"OK, OK," he said. "Flattery will get you somewhere. Brinkman got his money the old fashioned way, from his family. The old man was a Wall Street whiz who made a killing by duping unsuspecting little old ladies out of their Social Security, and passed it on to junior. And the apple didn't fall far from the tree, either. Little Paul decides it would be fun to run a newspaper, so he does a hostile takeover of one that's in trouble in California, builds it up, then branches out. A few years ago he senses the natural American bloodlust, so he relocates to Florida and goes into the tabloid business. His other holdings include majority shares in half a dozen or so tech companies, utilities, real estate and a few businesses in California."

"Would one of those be a company named Climaxxx Films?" Nick asked.

"If you knew all that, why did you call me?" Burke asked. "Yeah, that's one of his, but you won't see it on his annual report."

"What about his background?" Nick asked. "Any military ties?"

Burke leaned back and thought, searching his extensive memory.

"He served in Naval Intelligence during Viet Nam," he answered. "Rumor has it that he was involved in some controversial business in Saigon towards the end, but the whole thing was hushed up by the Pentagon."

"Can you find out what that incident was and what he's been up to lately?" Nick asked. "Any link to the CIA?"

"Man, that's YOUR beat," Burke answered. "If you want to know if Brinkman's on the CIA payroll, why not call them yourself?"

"Let's say I'm persona non grata with The Agency these days," Nick answered. "Can you find out for me?"

"Yeah, I can find out," Burke answered. "But like I said: what's in this for me?"

Nick thought for a minute before answering, taking a puff on his cigarette. This was one of those 'fight or flee' moments. He decided it was time to stop running.

"Do you remember those supposed terrorist attacks earlier this year including the courthouse bombing in Cleveland and the attempted robbery of the Federal Reserve in New York?" Nick asked.

"Yeah," Burke said, nodding his head in interest. "I

remember. The boys on The Hill were all up in arms about it. Really made your old boss jump through some hoops to explain how that happened on his watch. The Feds never did find the parties responsible. What about them?"

Nick looked Burke in the eyes.

"Suppose I told you who was really behind those attacks?" he asked. "You'd have an exclusive. Do we have a deal?"

Burke thought for a minute.

"Where can I reach you?" he finally asked.

Nick reached into his wallet and handed Burke one of his business cards.

"Do you have a private e-mail address?" Burke asked.

Nick wrote his home e-mail address on the back of the card.

"You can reach me there when you find out what I need. Will I hear from you soon?"

"That depends. Are you serious about knowing who pulled those jobs?" Burke asked.

Nick looked at Burke again.

"Dead serious," he said.

Nick's plane arrived in Miami at 4:45. He drove straight to Calhoun's, to see how business was on the first day they reopened after the fight of two days earlier. He was happy to see a full parking lot. He went inside and assumed his usual table overlooking the marina. Raul came over, and the two men chatted about the business of the day. Nick looked around the club.

"Where's Felicia?" he asked.

"Don't know, Chief," Raul answered. "She didn't show up tonight, and when I called your house, I kept getting a busy signal."

"When was the last time you called?" Nick asked suspiciously.

"About an hour ago. I was gonna try again, but we started getting busy."

Nick got up and quickly left the club. He sped out of the parking lot, almost hitting another car. Nick raced along Highway 1 towards his home, making the fifteen minute trip in less than ten. As he pulled into the parking lot of his complex, he turned off the headlights, and parked a few doors away from his condo. Opening the storage compartment in the console, he reached under some papers and withdrew a .38 revolver he kept there for emergencies. He got out of the car and quietly closed the door.

Nick cautiously approached his condo. The lights were on, but he could see no sign of movement through the front window. Going to the front door, he slowly tried the doorknob, and found it unlocked. He went to the left of the door, flattened himself against the wall, and slowly pushed the door open with his left foot. Hearing no response from inside, he crouched down and went in, sliding himself along the door, his gun drawn and pointed.

The living room had been searched, but nothing appeared broken or missing. Every drawer had been opened and the contents strewn about, and there were books and magazines on the floor. He slowly went into his den, and saw that his private lair had received the once-over. Every drawer and cubbyhole of the rolltop desk had been thoroughly, professionally searched.

There was no sign of Felicia, so he softly proceeded

upstairs to the master bedroom, his gun still drawn. Someone had been through this room, too, but it didn't appear that anything was missing. As he stood in the middle of the bedroom, he heard a muffled moaning sound coming from the closet. He opened the door, and found Felicia lying on the closet floor, her hands tied behind her back, a bandanna wrapped around her mouth as a gag, and a nasty-looking bump on her forehead. He quickly untied her and removed the gag, then dragged her out of the closet, laying her on the bedroom floor.

She was slowly regaining consciousness. Felicia looked up through half-open eyes, and squinted at Nick. A small smile creased her face.

"Hey, Tough Guy," she said weakly. "What took you so long?"

"I can't leave you alone for a minute," Nick responded, helping her to her feet and a nearby chair. He got her a glass of water from the bathroom.

"Did you see who did this?" he asked.

Felicia weakly shook her head 'no.'

"Stockin' mask," she replied. "Guy was five-ten, medium build, black windbreaker and pants, wearin' gloves. Anything missin'?"

"I don't think so," Nick replied. "Whatever he was looking for, I doubt he found it. But he trashed the place to make it look like a burglary."

"How'd you know I was here?" she asked.

"I went to the club. Raul said you didn't come in, and that he couldn't get an answer when he called."

"I got suckered," she said. "I was up here gettin' ready to go to work when this asshole sneaks up and grabs me.

I tried fightin' him off, but that's when he hit me with the butt end of his gun. I didn't even hear him come in."

"Do you remember what kind of gun?"

"Glock semi-auto," she replied.

"Standard Agency issue," Nick said, almost to himself.

"What?" Felicia asked.

"Nothing," Nick said, changing the subject. "We'd better have that bump looked at."

Felicia protested.

"No, Hon," she said. "Just get me an ice pack and some aspirin. I'll be OK."

"Like I always said," Nick stated, "Toughest broad this side of the West Indies."

Felicia started to laugh, then stopped, holding her head.

"Don't make me laugh," she said.

Nick gave Felicia pain killers and one of his phenobarbital tablets, and put her to bed. He then went downstairs to what was left of his den, called Raul at Calhoun's to tell him everything was OK and proceeded to put things back in order.

After accounting for everything, he got a glass of Scotch, put on some jazz CD's (he always relaxed when listening to Diana Krall and George Shearing), and sat down in the padded swivel chair in front of his desk. As he sat there and smoked, the more upset he got.

You went too far this time, he thought. *You invaded my home turf, and I can't let that pass.*

Nick was too keyed up to even think about going to bed. He fixed another drink and decided to log onto his computer and surf the Net, to catch up on what was going on elsewhere in the world. Nick was bored by most of what passed for entertainment on television, so he often preferred to hole up in his private sanctuary and pass time this way. He was reading the latest news on MSNBC when an item caught his eye. The Secretary of Defense had issued a statement to the media in response to questions about the Federal Government's inability to find and bring forth the people responsible for the terrorist attacks on American soil eight months earlier. The Secretary promised that this was an on-going investigation of the highest priority and that the perpetrators of these atrocities would soon be found and punished.

Nick shook his head slowly.

Maybe sooner than you think, he thought.

Nick was scanning the business section when his computer chimed, and the mailbox icon appeared, indicating that he had a new e-mail message.

It was from Dave Burke, starting off with a message that said, "When do I get my exclusive?" Nick then proceeded to read the attached pages that Burke had sent to him. There were six pages of information. Nick read it all, and found great interest in the last two pages. He re-read it several times, in disbelief, appreciating anew the chances Burke took in pursuing a story. This stuff was pure dynamite.

He printed all of the pages, then inserted a floppy disc into the computer and transferred the information onto the disc. Just for insurance, he repeated the procedure on a second disc, then locked both of them up in the safe he had hidden in the den.

Nick sat back in his chair and puffed on a cigarette. He was planning on how best to use the information Burke sent him. A grin started to slowly spread across Nick's face as he decided what to do.

Let's see how it feels to be on the receiving end for a change, he thought.

- *Fourteen* -

Paul Brinkman was on the phone in his office the next morning.

"Everything's going according to plan," he said. "I expect our friend to crack anytime now."

"Are you sure?"

Brinkman chuckled.

"With the pressure I've been putting on him, he can't last much longer."

"I'm glad to hear that. Just to be sure, though, I applied a little pressure myself."

Brinkman's face took on a frown.

"What do you mean?" he demanded. "I thought we agreed this was my operation."

"Just a little added incentive," the other party calmly replied. "I don't think Seven's going to appreciate having his girlfriend roughed up."

"Don't you know what that means?" Brinkman practically bellowed into the phone. "Now he'll think I did it and come after me!"

The person on the other end of the line chuckled.

"You shouldn't worry so much, Paul. You'll get ulcers. Besides, don't forget who's giving the orders. You just do as you're told."

Brinkman started to get his blood pressure back under control.

"All right," he finally said. "I won't forget again."

He hung up, leaned back in his upholstered leather chair, and wished the whole affair was over.

* * *

Back on Key Largo, Felicia was feeling better from her attack the night before. She and Nick sat on the deck drinking coffee and enjoying the start of the new day. Thanks to the sleeping pill, she had gotten a good night's sleep. Nick wished he could have said the same for himself. After reading the morning newspaper, Nick told Felicia about his e-mail from Dave Burke and showed her the pages he had printed. She read the documents word for word, shaking her head slowly in disbelief.

"Wow," she finally said. "What's your next move?"

"I think it's time I paid a visit to The Great Man myself," Nick said.

"What you gonna do when you get there?" she asked.

Nick looked at her for a moment, a slight smile curling his lips.

"Bluff," he answered.

Nick called Brinkman's office to make an appointment. The media mogul was only too happy to see him, probably figuring that Nick was ready to give up the fight. Before driving up to Miami, Nick prepared himself by putting on the wristwatch with the recorder hidden in the band, and stopping at the local Kinko's to make copies of the pages he had printed up the night before. The original copies he put into a manilla envelope, along with the photos and floppy discs he had accumulated, and addressed it to the bank in Barbados where he had sent the previous package, with a note to Felicia's brother to place the envelope in the safe deposit box with the other things he had sent. He paid the necessary postage, requested a return receipt upon delivery, and left the envelope with the clerk for pickup later that morning. Now it was time for the first showdown.

Nick was ushered into Brinkman's office, and offered a seat. Brinkman sat down behind the massive oak desk, a smug look on his face.

"Well," Brinkman began. "Have you come to make a deal?"

"Before I say anything, " Nick began, "turn off the camera and the tape recorder."

"What are you talking about?" Brinkman asked in total innocence.

"The camera that's in that sculpture behind your desk, and the tape recorder hidden inside this paperweight in front of me," Nick responded.

Brinkman let out a soft chuckle.

"I really could use a man like you in my organization," he said as he reached under the desk, and turned off the recording devices.

"All right, Mr. Seven," he continued. "We're all alone now. What do you have to say for yourself?"

"Are you really planning on running an exposé on the CIA?" Nick asked.

"Yes I am," Brinkman answered. "Should boost our circulation at least 20%."

"Then you'll want to include this in your article," Nick said, opening the envelope and removing some papers.

Brinkman sat back in his chair and smiled in smug satisfaction, thinking he had scored another in the win column. Nick began reading from the first page.

"Paul Eldon Brinkman, Jr." he began. "Age 58. Owner of Brinkman Enterprises. Last year's reported income, 1.5 million dollars. Also owns one-third of Horizon Communications, twenty-five percent of Pacific Gas and Electric, plus numerous smaller holdings, including complete ownership of Climaxxx Films of San Francisco, a producer and distributor of adult-oriented video tapes. Married twice, no children."

He stopped reading and looked up at Brinkman.

"Which explains the appearance of Monica Foxx – with two x's – posing as Jennifer Brinkman, who never existed," he said

Brinkman's expression had taken on a slight change. He was still smiling smugly, but his eyes had narrowed as he stared at Nick.

"There's more," Nick continued. "Brinkman junior served in the Navy during the Vietnam war, spending the last three years of a six year hitch in Naval Intelligence, leaving the service with the rank of Lt. Commander. Named by an anonymous witness as the triggerman in the execution-style slaying of Phong Luc, a suspected Viet Cong spy, in Saigon, December, 1971."

Nick stopped reading, and looked at Brinkman. His expression had completely changed to one of shock, and all the color had drained from his face. Nick thought the old guy was going to throw up. Suddenly the Big Man didn't look so intimidating.

"What do you want?" Brinkman asked, almost in a hoarse whisper.

"Who was the anonymous witness who fingered you for the killing of that spy in Saigon?" Nick asked.

Brinkman paused, and licked his suddenly dry lips before answering.

"Daniel Currey," he finally answered. "He was my superior in Intelligence at the time, and he ordered me to execute Phong Luc. Said it would serve as an example for the other spies we were interrogating."

"That explains the note on your calender to "Call DC," Nick said. "I also have phone records to verify that call, plus all the other conversations you two had, along with photographs of Currey visiting you on Singer Island last week. Was it Currey's idea for you to put the squeeze on me?"

Brinkman had broken out into a cold sweat.

"Yes," he answered. "He told me if I didn't do it, he'd re-open the Saigon business and have me indicted for murder under the old War Crimes act."

"So Currey sent you my personnel file?" Nick persisted.

Brinkman suddenly looked exhausted.

"Yes," he wearily replied. "Currey said to use it against you any way I could."

"What did he say he wanted from me?"

"I don't know," Brinkman answered in the same weary tone. "Only that you had some information he wanted, you wouldn't give it to him, and for me to put pressure on you until you caved in."

"So you set all this up yourself," Nick said. "The phony blackmail scheme, the visit from the INS, the girl in my bar, the truckers who staged that fight, Harry Trent's murder, having someone break into my house and beat up my girlfriend – that was all your doing?"

"No," Brinkman said, vigorously shaking his head. "Not all of it. The blackmail, the INS, the girl in the bar and the fight were mine, but not Trent's murder, and not the break-in or the attack. I had nothing to do with those."

"Did you send those two cops to grill me about Trent's murder?"

Brinkman nodded his head weakly.

"I had a photographer following you," he replied. "Currey called me when Trent was killed and when I saw the picture of you leaving his office building I called the police and gave them your name."

"And you had someone leave those pictures at my front door?"

Brinkman nodded weakly again. Nick paused for a moment, taking in everything Brinkman had said.

"What – what are you going to do with that?" Brinkman stammered, pointing to the papers in Nick's hands.

Nick paused again, thinking.

"I'm not sure," he answered. "Tell me – how would you like to get out from under, and get even at the same time?"

Brinkman eyed him suspiciously.

"How?" he finally asked.

"Say nothing to anyone – I mean anyone – about my visit here today or what I shared with you," Nick said.

"Don't call anyone in Washington, not even a coded e-mail message, and I'll tear this up and give you your insider's account on The Agency. That should be good for at least a 30% boost, wouldn't you say?"

Brinkman weakly nodded, experiencing the sting of defeat for the first time.

The next morning, Nick was back in Washington. He had made two phone calls the day before, and was on his way to his first appointment at CIA Headquarters. He had to pay a visit to an old friend while he was in town. Before leaving Key Largo, Nick transferred Brinkman's confession from the wristband recorder to a micro-cassette, and made additional copies of the pictures, tapes and documents. He also transferred part of Brodie's confession onto another tape.

Daniel Currey was expecting him. Nick was ushered into his high-security office, where he took a seat across from his former boss. It isn't often a man gets to stare down his fate. Nick was going to enjoy this.

"Well, Nick," Currey cordially began. "It's been a long time since we've seen each other."

"You're half right," Nick replied. "It's been a long time since you've seen me, but not so long since I saw you."

Currey stared at him curiously.

"Really?" he asked in feigned surprise. "When was that?"

"A few days ago, on Singer Island near Palm Beach," Nick answered. "Specifically, on the estate of Paul Brinkman."

Currey eyed him warily.

"I'm afraid you're mistaken," he said. "I haven't been

to Florida in months."

Nick opened the manilla envelope he brought in with him, and withdrew the photographs he had taken from his boat that afternoon. He laid them on Currey's desk.

"That's you in those pictures, Dan," Nick stated.

Currey looked at the photographs.

"So what?" he asked. "These don't prove anything."

"No," Nick agreed, "by themselves, they don't. But this might."

He withdrew a micro-cassette recorder from his breast pocket, and played back Brinkman's confession that he had secretly recorded the day before. When Brinkman's statement was done, Nick turned off the tape.

"Care to try again, Dan?" Nick asked. "I also have phone records of every call placed between you and Brinkman immediately before and after each act of aggression against me. Your move."

Currey looked at Nick, not sure whether to be angry or congratulate himself on the superior job he had obviously done in training the former agent years before. He picked up a pencil and began slowly tapping it on his desktop.

"All right, Nick," he finally said. "I think we've reached what they call an impasse. What is it you want?"

Nick pointed his right index finger at Currey.

"The reign of terror you're conducting on me stops – NOW," Nick said. "No more hassles, and you leave me and Felicia Hagens alone – permanently."

"You've forgotten something, Nick," Currey countered. "You still have information about Brodie's killing and those terrorist attacks that I want. And I'm prepared to get it – at any cost."

181

"Fine," Nick said. "Then we'll call the Attorney General."

"And say what?"

"That you engineered this whole thing, and coerced a private citizen into doing your dirty work for you."

"What private citizen?"

"Paul Brinkman. You heard him confess that this was all your idea, and that you blackmailed him into cooperating. You can also add a little charge of espionage, since you sent him classified documents."

"What classified documents?"

Nick looked hard at Currey.

"My personnel file," he replied.

Currey chuckled softly.

"You don't really think you're going to walk out of this building with that information, do you?" he asked.

"And you don't really think I'd be stupid enough to bring the only copies I have in here with me, do you?" Nick countered. "You trained me too well for that, Dan."

Currey said nothing, thinking about what Nick had said. He continued tapping the pencil.

"Just one other thing I have to know," Nick continued. "Why kill Harry Trent, and why have someone break into my home and beat up Felicia?"

Currey stopped tapping the pencil before answering.

"Trent was weak," Currey answered. "He was giving you information, and had to be taken out before he gave you enough to make the connection to Brinkman. The break-in and attack at your house was just to put more pressure on you. And I wouldn't count on getting any more favors from Bones McCoy, either."

"Did you have him killed, too?"

"No," Currey answered, "but I'm sure the Colombians have caught up with him by now, especially when word got to them that McCoy was the one who closed down their operation in Atlanta a few days ago. That's why I sent him down there on that suicide mission. Face it, Nick – all your friends are dropping like flies, and pretty soon, it'll be just you and me."

Nick paused for a moment, thinking about Bones.

One more for the undertaker, he cynically thought. *Lucky Nick strikes again.*

"You know what your problem is, Dan?" Nick asked. "You were always a lousy gambler – you never learned when to fold. Now, if I were you, I would seriously consider cutting my losses and getting out – while I still had that silk shirt on my back."

Nick stood up.

"It's time to retire, Dan," he said as he turned to leave the office.

"I still want what you have on Brodie and those attacks," Currey called after him.

Nick stopped, turned around and looked at him, shaking his head in amazement.

"You'll never learn," he answered, leaving the office.

Two hours later, Nick walked into Duke Ziebert's, and found Dave Burke at his usual booth, getting a jump on Happy Hour with the Martini in front of him. Nick sat down in the booth, and dropped the large envelope on the table.

"What's this?" Burke asked.

"The exclusive I promised you," Nick answered.

Burke eagerly reached for the envelope, but Nick pulled it back.

"One condition," Nick said.

"I'm listening," Burke answered.

"My name stays out of this – completely," he said, "or the deal's off and I take this to the New York Times."

"What if my editor asks me where I got my information?" Burke asked.

"Tell him I'm one of those 'well-placed anonymous sources' you guys are always blaming things on," Nick answered. "Deal?"

Burke nodded in the affirmative.

"Deal," he said.

Nick released his grip on the envelope, and Burke tore into it like a kid opening presents on Christmas. Nick sat back, ordered coffee and lit a cigarette as Burke read the contents. A smile started to appear on Burke's face as he read the documents and examined the photographs. Nick had outlined both Brinkman's and Currey's involvement in his current woes, as well as Trent's murder, the execution of Phong Luc, and the record of phone calls between the two men.

"Can this stuff on Brinkman be corroborated?" Burke asked after he finished reading.

"Listen for yourself," Nick replied, as he took out the tape recorder and played the same section of tape he played for Currey hours earlier. Burke listened, and let out a low whistle.

"What about Currey?"

Nick continued playing the tape, which contained his conversation with Currey, having recorded it from the wristband recorder on his way to the restaurant. Burke shook his head in amazement.

"Unbelievable," Burke said. "So the big guy used the cover of his office to kill one civilian and blackmail another. But this still doesn't explain those terrorist attacks."

Nick put another cassette in the tape recorder and replayed the part of his interrogation of Brodie in London six months earlier, where Brodie admitted setting up the attacks.

"Who was that?" Burke anxiously asked.

"Gene Brodie, Bureau Chief of Domestic Affairs for the Agency," Nick replied.

Burke's eyes widened slightly.

"Hey," he said, "wasn't he the agent they found assassinated in England a few months back?"

Nick slowly nodded his head in the affirmative.

"So he was behind those attacks while working for the CIA," Burke said. "Did the Agency drop the hammer on him to take him out of commission, then cover up the whole thing?"

Nick looked at Burke for a moment. A small grin creased his face and he chuckled softly.

"I always said you were a sharp reporter, Dave," he replied.

"Any chance I can have those for authenticity?" Burke asked.

Nick handed the tapes to Burke.

"Those are copies," he said. "The originals and other copies are stashed in a safe place. That's my personal insurance policy. And remember – I'm an anonymous voice on those tapes. Right?"

"Right," Burke said.

"With what I've given you today, you should have a couple weeks worth of material," Nick said. "Of course, you may have to go before another Federal Grand Jury."

Burke gave a short laugh.

"Screw them," he replied. "Looks like I'd better get back to the office and rewrite tomorrow's column before deadline. Nick, I really owe you."

"Forget it," Nick said. "Just send me a bottle of Scotch when you pick up your Pulitzer. Actually, you're lucky. I only gave this story to you because I like you. I made the same deal with Brinkman yesterday."

Burke laughed.

"You're kidding!" he exclaimed. "Are you going to tell him the deal's off?"

Nick slowly shook his head.

"I'll let him read about it in the paper," he said.

The next morning, Nick picked up a copy of The Washington Post on his way to Calhoun's. When he got there, he quickly turned to "Burke's Beat" on page four. There it was, for all the world to see – "CIA Chief and Media Mogul Implicated in Coverups and Killings." Nick chuckled as he read the article, which not only detailed the plot hatched by Currey and Brinkman, but pointed the finger of blame for the terrorist attacks squarely at the CIA, stating that one of their operatives had planned and executed the attacks, which were then covered up by the Agency. Nick laughed out loud when he read the words "according to a knowledgeable source." At the end of the article Burke promised continuing coverage of this outrageous abuse of government power.

The following afternoon found Nick in the marina, tinkering with his boat, when Felicia called out to him from the deck of Calhoun's.

"Nick!" she called out excitedly. "You got to come in and see this!"

Nick hurriedly went into the bar, where the television was tuned in to CNN. The breaking story was out of Washington, and reported the indictment by a Federal Grand Jury of Paul Brinkman on charges of conspiracy to commit various felonies, and possible murder for the slaying of a Viet Cong national in 1971. There was accompanying footage of The Great Man being escorted from his office in handcuffs by Federal Marshals. There was also a related story that announced the sudden retirement of CIA Chief Daniel Currey after a long and distinguished career. As if that weren't enough, the President had held a press conference, announcing the appointment of a special committee to be headed by the Attorney General and the Justice Department to investigate the allegations brought forth in The Post, specifically the operations of the Central Intelligence Agency under Daniel Currey's leadership.

Nick smiled, got a drink from the bar, and went to his table. Felicia joined him.

"Ya know," she began, "I'd like to ask if you had anythin' to do with this, but if I do, you won't tell me, will you."

Nick sipped his drink before answering.

"Let's just say that I wrote to my representative in Washington," he answered.

"Then no more trouble?" she asked.

Nick slowly shook his head 'no.'

"And no more bad memories?" Felicia persisted.

Nick gazed into her soft brown eyes as a small smile slowly spread across his face.

"Only good ones – Mrs. Seven," he replied with a twinkle in his eye.

"Well, I'm glad it's over," she started to reply, stopping short when she realized what Nick had said. "What did you call me?"

"Mrs. Seven," Nick responded. "Unless, of course, you find the idea of spending the rest of your life here in paradise with me revolting."

Felicia got that lovely, embarrassed little-girl look on her face again, and looked down while absent-mindedly fixing her hair. After a moment, she looked up at Nick, smiling.

"For better or worse?" she asked.

"Better, better!" Nick answered.

*

Printed in the United States
20309LVS00004B/61